Rob's eyes darkened [...] head, touching his l[...] with a sigh he closed the gap and pulled her against him. He lifted his head and stared down at her with wild, tortured eyes.

"Come back to me, Maisie," he said softly, his voice roughened with a need so intense it made her legs buckle.

She closed her eyes and felt a tear squeeze out from under one lid and slide slowly down her cheek. "Oh, Rob, I can't. Don't ask that of me, please. It would be so easy, but we can't go there. Not now. I can't let you hurt me again—"

"No! Maisie, no, I don't want to hurt you. I never wanted to hurt you. It was just the wrong time for us."

"And it's still the wrong time, Robert. We've got a wedding to get through. I can't deal with this complication now."

"And after the wedding? What then, my love?"

"I don't know," she said, her voice little more than a whisper. "Ask me then."

Dear Reader,

When my daughter phoned me (in the supermarket!) to tell me that her boyfriend had proposed, it was hardly a surprise, but still in some ways a shock. Not so the very highly organized way she tackled the wedding planning, and the great fun and fraught emotions and stress that paved the journey. But it was all worth it; the wedding, when it came, was a beautiful, memorable day that will live with me forever. She was utterly radiant, didn't stop smiling for the entire day, and it was wonderful. My husband's speech recalled things we'd remembered together, and it dawned on me how lucky we were still to be together. And when my editor said, "Caroline, we'd like you to write a book about a mother and her daughter both making this journey together," it seemed only natural that the hero should be the bride's father, as well, because they would be forced together to plan the wedding, and in the course of it would have to confront their own failed relationship and rebuild a new one—after all, some day they'd be grandparents. And when, on the way, each of them realizes they're still in love...well, you'll have to read it!

I hope you enjoy this momentous journey as much as I did. Have a wonderfully happy Mother's Day!

Love,

Caroline

CAROLINE ANDERSON

Mother of the Bride

HARLEQUIN®

TORONTO • NEW YORK • LONDON
AMSTERDAM • PARIS • SYDNEY • HAMBURG
STOCKHOLM • ATHENS • TOKYO • MILAN • MADRID
PRAGUE • WARSAW • BUDAPEST • AUCKLAND

Recycling programs
for this product may
not exist in your area.

ISBN-13: 978-0-373-74028-4

MOTHER OF THE BRIDE

First North American Publication 2010.

Copyright © 2010 by Caroline Anderson.

Caroline Anderson has the mind of a butterfly. She's been a nurse, a secretary and a teacher, has run her own soft-furnishing business, and now she's settled on writing. She says, "I was looking for that elusive something. I finally realized it was variety, and now I have it in abundance. Every book brings new horizons and new friends, and in between books I have learned to be a juggler. My teacher husband, John, and I have two beautiful and talented daughters, Sarah and Hannah, umpteen pets and several acres of Suffolk that nature tries to reclaim every time we turn our backs!"

Praise for Caroline Anderson

"Well-written characters locked in a plausible conflict will keep readers turning the pages— and pulling for a successful reunion."
—*RT Book Reviews* on *Two Little Miracles*

For my darling daughter Sarah,
for providing me with so much source material and
inspiration, and for Adam, who had the foresight
to anticipate this book and ask her to marry him!
Thank you both for the most wonderful day,
and here's to many, many happy years ahead.

And for all the other mothers-of-the-bride with
whom I've shared the journey: Petrice, Carol,
Elizabeth, Dee, Linda and Thila, with my love.

CHAPTER ONE

'MAISIE.'

Just the one word, but it curled around her, invading every part of her, swamping her with its gruff warmth. Her heart went into overdrive, her breath stalling at the unaccustomed and yet, oh, so familiar sound of his voice. And then fear kicked in.

'Rob, what is it? What's happened?'

'Nothing's happened—yet,' he said quietly. 'I just wanted to warn you, Alec's going to ask Jenni to marry him this evening, and he wanted my blessing. I thought you should know.'

So the time had come. Maisie's heart sank. For the last three years, ever since her baby had started dating the gentle, humorous Alec Cooper with his smouldering eyes and teasing sense of fun, she'd been waiting for this moment, and now it was here. Her legs felt like jelly, her heart was pounding, her mouth was dry, and she wanted to scream, *'No! She's too young! Don't let her, she's not ready…'*

'Maisie?'

'I'm OK,' she said, sitting down abruptly on the edge of the bed. The bed in which she'd given Rob her virginity over twenty-one years ago.

'Are you sure?'

'Sort of. Thank you for warning me, although it would have been nice if Alec had done it,' she said.

'I know,' he said, his voice sympathetic. 'I suggested he should, but he was afraid you'd try and warn Jenni off.'

'Rob, I'm her *mother*!'

'Exactly. And you have…'

'Issues?' she offered into the silence, and he gave a quiet huff of laughter that clawed at her insides.

'You could put it that way. I told him you'd be upset, but he was very reluctant in case you tried to speak to Jenni, to talk her out of it, because he's been planning it for ages, apparently, and he was desperate for it to be a surprise.'

'Rob, he should have spoken to me, too. I'm the one who's brought her up. Or doesn't my blessing count?'

His sigh was soft. 'Maisie, don't be like that. I asked him to talk to you, he said he'd think about it, but obviously he didn't feel he could, or he hasn't been able to get you. He asked me not to tell you until he had time to ask Jenni, and he's doing that now, as we speak, so I couldn't tell you any sooner. I gave him my word. You have to respect that.'

Of course she did. She just felt out of the loop, as usual, at the bottom of the heap when it came to knowing anything, and it hurt. 'It doesn't matter,' she lied, but he cut in gently.

'It does—and I'm really sorry. If it helps, he only asked me about four hours ago. And my mother doesn't know.'

A small crumb of comfort, but surprisingly perceptive of him to know she'd needed it.

She closed her eyes and gave a tiny, shaky little laugh. 'Rob, they're so young.'

'They'll be fine. I'm sure Jenni'll ring you the moment they're back. It might be nice if you act surprised.'

She swallowed. 'Sure—and, Rob… Thank you for warning me.'

'It's a pleasure,' he said, his voice low and gruff, and she felt the familiar shiver down her spine.

How could he still do that to her, after all these years? She should have got over him by now. She said goodbye and replaced the phone in the cradle, and sat staring at the wall blankly. It really was going to happen. Jenni and Alec were getting married, and even though she'd known it was coming, she was still reeling with shock.

'You're being ridiculous,' she told herself, and,

getting up, she went back over to her wardrobe and carried on the weeding process she'd been engaged in when Rob had called.

She pulled out a hanger and stared at it blankly. Good grief, how ever long had she had these trousers? Far too long, she hadn't worn them for years. She dumped them on the growing pile, found a few other things and then realised she'd put her favourite dress on the pile by accident.

She wasn't with it at all, she was miles away, in Scotland, with Jenni, praying that common sense would prevail and she'd tell Alec they should wait. Hoping it would work for them. Worried that it wouldn't, that like their marriage, Jenni's would prove too frail to stand the test of time.

They'll be fine.

Would they? She didn't know, but Rob's deep, warm voice echoed in her ears, and if she let herself, she could almost believe it. But not quite, because he'd said the same thing to her over twenty-one years ago, when he'd asked her to marry him.

'We'll be fine, Maisie. You'll see. It'll be all right.'

But it hadn't been. It hadn't been all right at all, in the end, even though the beginning had been blissful. Stormy, sometimes, but they'd always, always made up after a row, and sometimes she wondered if they'd had fights just for the hell of it, so they could make up afterwards.

She laughed at the memory, but her smile faded and she felt her eyes fill.

She'd married him not only because she loved him, but also because she'd been eighteen, scared, pregnant, and her family wanted nothing to do with her. Her options had been severely restricted, and she'd thought he loved her as much as she'd loved him, but she'd been wrong. She must have been. If he'd loved her, he'd have come after her, but he hadn't, so she'd concluded sadly that he'd only married her out of duty, when they'd hardly known each other—certainly not well enough to weather the birth of Jenni while he was away at sea and she was alone in Scotland with his less-than-enthralled parents.

It wasn't really surprising that it hadn't worked, under the circumstances. They'd been children, out of their depth in the welter of emotions they'd encountered, coping with a situation that would have challenged anyone. And when she couldn't bear it any more up there without him, when she'd left Scotland and come back down here to Cambridge, he'd done nothing about it, to her horror and distress. There had just been a terrible, deafening silence.

He hadn't come to her when he'd had his next shore leave, as she'd expected, hadn't tried to find out what was wrong, but had said nothing, done nothing for six whole months except send money to her account. She'd taken it because she'd had no choice, and she'd written to him begging him to come to her, to talk to her—anything, but there'd been no reply, and then at last there had been a letter asking for access to Jenni in their divorce settlement—a divorce that hadn't even been on her agenda until he'd broached the subject. Shocked, devastated, she'd agreed to everything he'd asked, and the only contact they'd had since then had been over Jenni.

She'd hardly seen him in all this time—scarcely at all since Jenni had grown old enough to spend time with him alone without needing her, and certainly not at all in the last five years. They hardly even spoke on the phone any more. There was no need. If there was anything relating to Jenni, it was discussed with her directly, which was why his call today out of the blue had been so shocking.

She couldn't remember the last conversation they'd had that had lasted more than a very few seconds, but she guessed they'd be having to talk to each other now, and the thought brought all her confused and tumbled emotions about him racing to the surface. Emotions she'd never dealt with, just closed off behind a wall of ice in her heart before they destroyed her.

She still loved him, she realised. She'd die

loving him, but it was a one-sided, unrequited love that had never stood a chance. And she was far too old to be so foolish.

The phone rang again, and for a moment she stared at it, her heart pounding, knowing who it was, knowing what she was about to hear, but stalling anyway because until she heard it, it might not be true…

'Mummy?'

'Hello, darling. How are you?'

'Amazing! You'll never guess what—are you sitting down?'

She wasn't, but she did. Rapidly. 'OK. Fire away, what's happened?' she said, trying to sound fascinated and intrigued and enthusiastic instead of just filled with a sense of doom. She'd seen the look in Jenni's eyes, and Alec reminded her so much of Rob as he had been—young, eager, in love—

'Alec's asked me to marry him!'

She squeezed her eyes shut briefly and sucked in a breath. Hard. Her lungs were jammed up tight, her heart was in the way and she wanted to cry.

She didn't. She opened her eyes, forced a smile and said, 'Oh, my goodness—so what did you say?' As if she didn't know what the answer would have been…

Jenni laughed, her happiness radiating unmistakeably down the phone line. *My baby. My precious, precious baby.*

'*Yes*, of course! What on earth did you expect me to say? Mummy, I *love* him! You're supposed to be pleased for me! You *are* pleased for me, aren't you?'

There was a note of uncertainty, of pleading, and Maisie sat up straighter and forced some life into her voice. 'Oh, darling, of *course* I am—if it's what you really want…'

'You know it's what I want. I love him, and I want to be with him forever.'

'Then congratulations,' she said softly. And then, pretending she didn't already know, she added, 'I wonder what your father will say?'

'Oh, he's really happy for us.'

'That's good.' Her voice sounded hollow, echoing in her ears, but Jenni laughed again, unaware of Maisie's inner turmoil.

'Alec asked him first, apparently. They're really close, and he wanted his blessing—it's so like him. He really wanted to do it right, and I had absolutely no idea. It was amazing. He took me up to the ruin and got down on one knee—and I just burst into tears. I think he was a bit shocked.'

'I'm sure he wasn't, he knows you better than that. So, when are you talking about? Next year? The year after?'

'As soon as I graduate—we thought maybe the third Saturday in June, if the church is free?'

'But, Jenni, that's only a few weeks!' she said, her mind whirling. Surely not—please, no, that would be too ironic if Jenni, too…

'Ten and a half—but that's fine. We want to get it over before the really busy summer season, and the weather will be best then. If we wait until autumn the weather up here could be cold and wet and awful.'

'Up there?' she said, the timescale forgotten, blanked out by this last bombshell.

'Well—yes, of course up here, Mum! It's where I live now, where everyone is, except you. We're all here.'

Jenni was right, of course, and she should have seen it coming. They all did live up there, light years away in the wild and rugged West Highlands. Everyone except her. Jenni's fiancé Alec, his family, Jenni's uni friends in Glasgow, Alec's friends—and Jenni's father.

Robert Mackenzie, Laird of Ardnashiel, king of his castle—literally. And she'd been nothing, a nobody; in the words of the taunting kindergarten rhyme, the dirty rascal, the girl who'd got herself knocked up with the heir's baby and then, little more than a year after their wedding, had walked away. Why had he let her go without a murmur, without coming after her, without trying to fix what was surely not that broken? She didn't know. She might never know.

And now her darling daughter—*their* daughter—was getting married, in the very church where she and Rob had made their vows over twenty years ago. Vows that had proved as insubstantial as cobwebs…

She shuddered and sucked in a breath, the silence on the phone hanging in the air like the blade on a guillotine.

'Mum?'

'Yes, darling. Sorry. Of course you're having it there,' she agreed, squashing the regret that she wouldn't be married here, in Cambridge, from the home where she'd grown up. But that was unrealistic, and she was sensible enough to recognise that now. 'Where else, when you've got such a lovely setting? But—only ten and a half weeks?' she said, her voice perilously close to a squeak of dismay as she thought of the reasons that might exist for their haste. 'Don't you need longer to plan it?' she hedged.

The lovely ripple of her daughter's laughter made Maisie want to cry again. 'Oh, it's all planned! We're having the wedding here in the church, of course, and the hotel in the village can do the catering. They've got a brilliant restaurant, so the food will be great. And we'll have a marquee on the lawn and if it rains there's plenty of room inside, and we can have a ceilidh in the ballroom—it'll be wonderful! But you have to come now, because I need a dress and I've only got a week and a bit before I have to go back to uni, and you *have* to help me choose it. And we have to look for something for you, too—you'll need something really lovely, and I want to be there when you choose it. I need you, Mum. Say you'll come.'

Her voice had dropped, sounding suddenly hesitant, and Maisie knew she had no choice. *Wanted* no choice. This was her baby, her only child, and she was getting married, whether Maisie liked it or not.

'Of course I'll come,' she said, squashing down her apprehension and concentrating on being positive. 'I wouldn't miss it for the world.'

'Great. I can't wait, it's going to be such fun! Look, I have to go, we've got to tell Alec's parents before they go to bed, but I'll hand you over to Dad. He wants to talk to you.'

Oh, lord. Not now. Please, not now, not again. She needed to crawl under the covers and have a really good howl, and the last thing she needed to do was make small talk with the man who still held her heart in the palm of his hand.

'She wants me to come up,' she told him, sticking firmly to business.

'Yes. It needs to be soon, so I hope you aren't too busy. When are you free?'

Never. Not to go there, to the chilly, forbidding castle, with his mother still there despising her and him indifferent to her feelings, doing what was right instead of what mattered and riding rough-shod over her heart. Except apparently he wasn't indifferent to her feelings any more. Maybe he'd grown up. Twenty years could do that to you.

'It's not too bad for the next couple of weeks. I interviewed someone today for a feature that I have to write up, and I'm doing a wedding tomorrow—'

'Can't you hand it over to someone?'

She shook her head. 'No. Not this one.'

'Why not? Surely some other photographer...'

She sucked in a breath, stunned that he could dismiss her so easily, implying that any photographer could do the job as well, as if it was just a case of pressing the right button at the right time. So much for him not being indifferent to her feelings!

'I don't think you quite understand the process,' she said drily, hanging onto her temper. 'Quite apart from the fact that they want *me*, not *some other* photographer,' she told him, 'you have to understand that brides are very emotional and there's no way I'd let her down at this point. I gave them my word—to quote you. And you have to respect that.'

There was a heartbeat of silence, then a quiet sigh. 'All right. So you have to do the wedding. What time will you be through?'

'Five? Maybe six, at the latest. It's in Cambridge, so it's local.'

'So—if you get the seven-fifteen from Cambridge to King's Cross tomorrow night, you can pick up the Deerstalker from Euston that gets to Fort William at ten the next morning. Will that be OK?'

The overnight sleeper? It would cost an arm and a leg—but she'd do it, for Jenni. 'Yes, I'll book it.'

'I've done it. I'm doing it on line now. I'll have the tickets waiting for you at the station to collect, and I'll pick you up in Fort William the day after tomorrow. And, Maisie?' he added, his voice dropping.

'Yes?'

'I know this is going to be difficult for you. It'll be difficult for me, too, but we have to do this for Jenni.'

'Of course we do,' she said wearily. 'And it'll be fine. I just wish I felt they were doing the right thing.'

'It is the right thing. It'll be all right, Maisie. You'll see.'

Those words again, echoing back at her over the years, reminding her of just how frail a thing love could be under pressure. She hoped he was right— heavens, how she hoped it, but she wouldn't bank on it. They were so young, so eager, so unaware of all the pain…

'I'll see you at ten on Thursday,' she said, and switched the phone off.

Thursday morning. Only—she glanced at her watch—thirty-six hours away. No time at all to shore up her defences and get her armour plating up and running.

She'd need days—

Ridiculous. She hadn't done it in twenty years, what made her think a few more days could make any difference?

She got off the bed—the very bed where he'd loved her so tenderly, so sweetly, so patiently. So skilfully. She stroked the quilt smooth, her mind back in the long-ago days when love had been sweet and laughter had been the order of the day.

She'd been about to start her degree here at the local college—not as prestigious as one of the Cambridge University colleges, of course, but it offered a good degree in journalism—and she had needed accommodation. Cheap accommodation. And Rob, who had just graduated with flying colours from one of the Cambridge colleges, had been looking for someone to share his house. He was off to serve in the Royal Navy, a six-year commission, and he needed a caretaker, all running expenses paid in return for maintaining the house in good condition in his absence.

Only one proviso—she had to live in it alone and share it with him occasionally when he was on shore leave, but that suited her fine, because it was the only way she could afford it and it meant she could get away from home, from a repressive father who didn't think she needed to go away to college.

So she'd arranged to view it, and they'd gone out for a drink to discuss the fine detail. Well, that had been the excuse. In fact, they'd just wanted to spend time together, and over the next few days they'd fallen headlong in love. Just a week after they'd met, she'd ended up here in this room, in this bed, giving him her heart.

He still had it. He always would.

She sighed and turned her back on the bed. She wanted nothing more than to crawl under the quilt and cry her eyes out, but she had a feature to write up before tomorrow, clothes to pack for her trip, a wedding to prepare for—and besides, she was all done crying over Robert Mackenzie. She'd worn that particular T-shirt out long ago, and she wasn't going there again.

* * *

'How do you think she took it?'

Badly. Especially when he'd implied that another photographer could step into her shoes at a moment's notice. He'd have to do better than that, Rob thought ruefully.

He smiled at his daughter—his beautiful, clever, radiantly happy daughter—and lied. 'She's fine,' he told her. 'I've booked her train ticket, and I'll pick her up—'

'Let me—please? Give me time with her, so I can talk her down a little. She'll be nervous.'

Nervous? Would she? Quite possibly, he conceded. 'She might not be very thrilled about it, but she's got nothing to be nervous about,' he said, trying to reassure their daughter.

But Jenni looked at him, wise beyond her years, and shook her head. 'Of course she has. She hated it here. She hasn't been here for twenty years and she'll be unsure of her welcome.'

'But—that's silly! She's your mother! Of course she's welcome,' he said, but then he thought about it, about the defensive tone of her voice, about how much she'd seemed to hate it here, and he sighed softly.

'I'll still pick her up. Even more reason. I can talk to her.'

Jenni chewed her lip. 'Dad—she won't want to talk to you. She goes out of her way to be out if you're coming to the house, she won't even look at you—what if she refuses to get in the car?'

'She won't refuse,' he said, wishing he was as certain as he sounded. 'She's not that fond of walking.'

Jenni gave a splutter of laughter and came over and hugged him, slapping him on the chest simultaneously. 'That was mean. You be kind to her or she'll end up in the hotel in the village, I know she will.'

'I'll be kind to her, Jenni,' he promised, serious now. 'I was always kind to her.'

'Were you? She's never really said anything very much about you, just that it didn't work out.'

'That's about the size of it,' he said, carefully keeping his voice neutral. 'But don't worry. We can do this. It'll be fine, Jenni.'

'Are you sure? You'll probably fight like hell. I don't think you know her. She seems like a pussy-cat, but she can be pretty feisty, you know.'

He laughed, but her words echoed in his head. Feisty? Oh, yes, she'd been feisty, but that wasn't how he remembered her. He remembered her *after* their fights—sweet, tender, passionate—until the end. Then she'd just been withdrawn and uncommunicative, as if all the spark had gone out of her, and he hadn't known how to get through to her. Jenni was right. He really didn't know her, the woman who'd been his wife, who'd taken his heart and broken it into little pieces...

'I'm sure we can be adult about it,' he said, not at all convinced but hoping it was true.

Jenni tipped her head on one side. 'Why did neither of you ever get married again? I mean, I know why you didn't stay married to each other, it's not rocket science, but why didn't you marry anyone else? It's not as if you're hideous, either of you, and you're both so nice.'

He shrugged, not intending to drag his wounds out into the open for his daughter to pick the scabs off. 'Never got round to it, I suppose,' he said casually. 'First I was in the navy, and then I was juggling establishing my business in London and being a father to you, and then my own father died and I had to move up here and take over the estate. And it's hard to meet anyone when you're up here in the backwaters, especially if you work in an almost exclusively male environment. Bear in mind that the majority of women who come to the estate are partners of men who come for the sport. They aren't looking for a husband.'

'Are you sure? Maybe they want to switch husbands? And anyway, that's rubbish. It's never hard to meet people when you're rich, it's just hard to meet the right people,' she said drily, and he could tell from her tone that there was a wealth of hurt there. She'd encountered some gold-diggers at uni, men who'd only been interested in her for her inheritance, she'd told him, but Alec, fiercely protective, had been there for her through thick and thin, and he knew the young man loved his daughter from the bottom of his kind and generous heart.

If only they'd been so lucky, him and Maisie. If only they'd found a love like that. It might not be rocket science, but it was a mystery to him why they hadn't got on. It had been so good at first, so special. Nothing had ever felt like it since, and that, of course, was why he'd never married again. Because to be married to anyone other than his Maisie would have been a travesty, a betrayal of everything he stood for.

He swallowed and stepped back, gently disentangling himself from Jenni's embrace, and headed for the door. 'Sorry, sweetheart, I've got a million things to do. I'll see you for dinner.'

He went out, whistling the dogs, and headed down to the water. He needed a walk, a good, long stretch along the beach and then up over the headland, the point that gave Ardnashiel its prefix. There had been a hut there once, evidently, a shiel, which long ago had given way to the original castle, and he climbed the hill towards the ruins, needing the peace, the solitude that he would find there.

It was his retreat, the place he went to soothe his soul, the harsh wind and savage sea the only things wild enough to match the turmoil in his heart, but today they could do nothing to wipe out the memories of his love, here in this place, where he'd brought her so many times. And now, for the first time, she was coming back, not to him, but to the castle.

It was a step he hadn't been sure she'd ever take, but now she was, and in two days she'd be here.

His beloved, beautiful Maisie was coming home…

The train was on the platform as she collected her ticket, and she only just made it before the doors closed.

The wedding had gone on longer than she'd expected, and it had been harder than she'd imagined. She didn't know why—maybe because now she had become the mother of a bride, and could put herself in Annette's shoes, with the agony of her uncertain future. She'd had a health scare, and was facing a gruelling treatment regime over the next months and maybe years, but today had not been a day for dwelling on that. Today was her daughter's day, and Annette had been radiant.

'I'm so proud of her. Doesn't she look beautiful?' she'd said to Maisie in a quiet, private moment, a little oasis in the midst of the revelry, and Maisie's eyes had filled.

'Yes—yes, she does, she looks absolutely gorgeous, and so do you.'

Annette had met her eyes, her own distressed. 'Take plenty of photos,' she begged, and then added softly, 'Just in case.'

Maisie had swallowed. 'I will. I have. I've got some wonderful ones of you together, and I'll get them to you very soon.'

'Thank you,' Annette had said almost silently, and Maisie had held her gently and shared that quiet moment of knowledge that there might not be very much time left to her, and every second mattered.

So now, on the train to London, she was downloading the photos from her camera onto her laptop, then burning them onto several disks and labelling them. Thank God for mobile technology, she thought as she put the disks in the post on her way from King's Cross to Euston.

She was pleased with the photos. She'd go through them, of course, editing out the dross and cropping and tidying up the images so they could look at them on her website, and she'd produce an album with the family once they'd chosen the ones they wanted, but for now, at least, they'd get them in the raw form almost immediately to look through with Annette.

And hopefully, in the years to come, she'd be showing them to her grandchildren, but if not, at least they'd have a wonderful record of that beautiful day.

She blinked away the tears and stared out of the window of the sleeper at the passing lights. The cabin was claustrophobic—first class, the best it could be, but she was too full of emotion, from the wedding and from the task facing her, to sit still.

She locked up her cabin securely and went to the lounge to order food. She hadn't eaten at the wedding, and she'd had her hands full on the platform at Euston, and her blood sugar was through the floor.

Even so, she didn't touch her supper. Her stomach felt as if someone had tied a knot in it and she gave up and went back to her cabin, lying down on the narrow berth and staring at the window, watching the lights flash past as they moved through stations, but mostly it was dark, the velvety blackness of the countryside all-engulfing as the train carried her north towards Rob.

And Jenni. It was about Jenni, she reminded herself—Jenni and Alec. She had to keep focus, remind herself what she was doing this for, or she'd go crazy.

Actually, what she needed was sleep, not the constant rumble of the rails, the clatter of the points, the slowing and shunting and pausing while goods trains went past, until she thought she'd scream. It wasn't the train's fault. It was comfortable, private—as good as it could be. It was just that she didn't want to be on it, didn't want to be doing this, and the memories were crashing over her like a tidal wave.

She'd done it for the first time when she was pregnant, when she'd just finished her first year's exams at Cambridge and was heading up to Scotland to wait for the birth. She'd wanted to stay in Cambridge, in their little house, but Rob had insisted she should move up to the castle. 'You can be looked after there, and my parents will want to spend time with the baby,' he'd said and so, because he wasn't there to drive her this time, as he had every other time they'd been, because he was already away at sea, she'd got on the train, exhausted, aching, and by the time she'd reached Glasgow, she'd realised she was in labour.

She'd been taken straight to the hospital in Fort William, and the next few hours were still a blur in her mind, but as the train rolled on, she kept reliving it, snatches of the pain and fear, knowing Rob was at sea and wanting him, needing him with her. And when he'd come at last, weeks later, he'd been different—distant, almost as if he couldn't bring himself to touch her. She'd known then that there was something wrong, but they hadn't talked about it, just tiptoed carefully around the cracks in their relationship as if they weren't there. And then he'd gone away again, back to sea, and left her behind to face the cold, dark winter there without him.

She hadn't been able to do it. Leaving the castle, going back south to Cambridge—it had seemed such a sensible move, the only thing she could do to stay sane. It had never occurred to her that Rob wouldn't follow.

She turned over, thumped the pillow, squeezed her eyes shut and pulled the quilt over her head, but the images were still there, crowding into her head, keeping her awake.

She gave up in the end, sitting perched on the lid of the washbasin in the corner and staring out of the window as the dawn broke. The country-side was getting wilder, the hills higher, the gentle ripples in the landscape giving way to crumples and then sharp, jagged pleats as they went further north. It was stark, bleak, with a wild majesty that made something in her ache at the beauty of it, but it terrified her, too, because of all the memories it held for her.

She was washed and dressed before the attendant knocked on the door with her breakfast—a hot bacon roll, tea and some fruit salad—and she sat on the bunk staring out over the wild, untamed landscape as the train slowly wended its way around the hills to Fort William, stopping at every station on the way, tiny outposts of civilisation in the midst of barren wilderness.

Not long now, she thought, and her stomach rejected all thought of the bacon roll after the first bite. She was fraught with nerves, too tense to eat, so she sipped her tea as they climbed up onto the flat and desolate plateau of Rannoch Moor, picked at the fruit because it was ridiculous to have nothing, and then gathered her things together as they pulled into the station in Fort William.

And then, when it was too late to do anything about it, she glanced at the mirror and winced. She looked awful. Dark circles under her tired, strained eyes, her hair in wild red corkscrews, needing attention—she hated travelling, hated the rush and pressure and hanging about. And Ardnashiel was waiting.

I'm not ready for it! she wanted to wail, but she didn't, she just picked up her camera bag, slung it over her shoulder, picked up her laptop and her suitcase and got off the train.

It should be like *Brief Encounter*, she thought, all swirling steam and whistles, but it wasn't, it was loud and noisy, unintelligible and horribly familiar. She took a deep breath and looked up, and he was there, walking slowly towards her in jeans and a sweater, with his rangy, muscular limbs and broad, solid shoulders. His hair was touched with grey now, she noticed in surprise, crow's feet at the corners of his wary, slate-blue eyes, and when he smiled, the crow's feet crinkled and turned her legs to mush.

'Maisie,' he said, and his voice curled round her again, seeping into her heart and unravelling all her resolve.

'Hello, Rob. Here, you can make yourself useful,' she said, and handed over her luggage before he could do anything stupid like kiss her cheek and pretend they were friends.

'Is this all?'

'Three bags? Isn't that enough? I can tell what sort of women you've been mixing with, Mackenzie.'

His smile was wry. 'Yeah, your daughter. I've conveyed her and her clutter back and forth to uni for the last three years, remember. I know how you women travel.'

'I'm only here for a week—two weeks, max.'

'We'll see. Come on, then, let's head back.'

To Ardnashiel. Her heart thumped, and she bit her lip as he led her into the car park and plipped the remote control in his hand. Lights flashed on a car—low, sleek and expensive. She might have known. He'd always liked expensive cars. He stashed her belongings in the boot, then opened the door for her. 'Can I put the lid down, or do you want it up?' he asked as he slid in behind the wheel and turned to her.

She shrugged, unsurprised that the car was a convertible, a folding hard-top. He'd never been able to get enough fresh air. 'Whatever you like. My hair's a mess anyway. I need a shower.'

'You look fine, Maisie,' he said softly. More than fine. She looked—lovely. Wary, hesitant, out of her comfort zone, but lovely. And he wanted her to himself, just for a little bit longer.

He pressed the button to fold the roof and held her eyes. 'Do you fancy a coffee on the way?'

She frowned then gave a slight smile, the first one since she'd got off the train. 'Actually, that would be really nice. I didn't eat much yesterday—too busy. And I didn't really fancy breakfast. I'm starving.'

'OK. We'll do coffee. There's a lovely place opened since you were here last.'

'Rob, there's been time for dozens of places to open and shut since I was here last,' she pointed out, and he gave a quiet laugh.

'I know. It's been a long time.' Too long.

He started the engine then they purred softly

out of the car park and headed out on the road to Mallaig. The air was cool, but it was a beautiful day and the sun was shining, and she put her head back against the butter-soft leather of the seat and closed her eyes, but even so, she couldn't cut him out of her thoughts.

She was aware of every movement he made, every breath he took, every flex of his muscles. Not because she could hear, or see, but because she just *knew*. After all this time, she still knew, her body so aware of him that her nerves were screaming.

How on earth had she imagined she could do this?

CHAPTER TWO

SHE looked wonderful. Tired, with deep smudges under her eyes, but wonderful.

She wasn't asleep, just resting her eyes, but it meant he could look at her out of the corner of his eye without being seen. And he wanted to look at her. Ridiculously badly.

She looked just the same, he thought with a twist to his heart. Well, no, not *just* the same, because she was thirty-nine now and she'd been eighteen when they'd first met, but the years had been kind to her and if anything she was more beautiful than she'd been twenty years ago.

Her skin was like rich cream, smooth and silky, dusted with freckles, and he wondered if it would still smell the way it had, warm and fragrant and uncomplicated. Her hair, wild and untamed, was still that wonderful rich red, a dark copper that she'd passed on to Jenni but which in their daughter was mellowed by his dark-haired gene to a glorious auburn.

She had the temper to go with it, too, the feistiness Jenni had reminded him of. It was something that fortunately neither of them had handed on to their daughter, but although at first they'd had stand-up fights that had ended inevitably in bed with tearful and passionate reconciliation, by the end there'd been no sign of it. And he'd missed it. Missed the fights, missed the making up. Missed his Maisie.

He sighed and turned into the car park of the café overlooking the top of Loch Linnhe, and by the time he'd cut the engine she had her seat-belt undone and was reaching for the door handle.

She straightened up and looked around, giving him a perfect back view, her jeans gently hugging that curved, shapely bottom that had fitted so well in his hands…

'This looks nice.'

He swallowed hard and hauled in a breath. 'It is nice. It's owned by the people who run the hotel in the village. They've got a local produce shop here as well, selling salmon and venison and cheese and the like.'

'And insect repellent?'

He chuckled, remembering her constant battle with the midges. 'Probably.' He held the door, and she went in and sniffed the air, making him smile.

'Oh, the coffee smells good.'

'It is good. What are you having?'

'Cappuccino, and—they look tasty.'

'They are. Do me a favour and don't even ask about the calories.'

'Don't worry, I won't,' she vowed, making him laugh. 'I'm starving.'

He ordered the coffees and two of the trade-mark gooey pastries, and they headed for a table by the window. He set the tray down and eased into the seat opposite her, handing her her cup.

'So, how did the wedding go yesterday?'

A flicker of distress appeared in her moss-green eyes before she looked down at her coffee. She poked the froth for a moment. 'OK. Lovely. Very beautiful. Very moving. The bride's mother's not well—that's why I couldn't hand it over.'

He frowned. 'Why didn't they postpone it?'

'Because she's about to start chemo,' Maisie said softly. 'They had to rush the wedding forward, and the last thing I could do to them was upset them at this stage. They wanted me, they trusted me, and I'd promised.'

'Of course. I'm sorry, I didn't appreciate that at the time. I can quite see that you had to stay, and I'm sorry if I implied that anyone else could take over from you. Of course that isn't true, especially under those circumstances. You had no choice.'

She blinked. He'd really taken her comments on

board, if that was anything to go by, but she wasn't surprised. He'd always been one for doing the right thing—even when it was wrong...

'You'll be wanting to send them the images.'

'I've done it. I downloaded them on the train and posted them at Euston. Just in case...' She sighed softly as she broke off, biting her lip and thinking of Annette.

'Poor woman,' he murmured. 'It must have been hard for the family, dealing with all those emotions.'

She nodded, but then she went quiet, sipping her coffee, absently tearing up the pastry and nibbling at it. 'Rob, this wedding—are you sure it's right for them? They're so young.'

'Not that young.'

'They are! Just like we were. We were far too young.'

'You can't compare them to us. They're three years older than we were—'

'No. I was eighteen, she's twenty. That's only two years.'

'She's almost twenty-one. She'll be twenty-one by the wedding, and Alec will be twenty-four. And those years make a lot of difference. You were only just eighteen and pregnant, and I was twenty-one and committed to the navy for six years, and we didn't know each other nearly well enough.'

'We still don't.'

'No. Jenni said that on Tuesday, and I think she was right. But they're different, Maisie. They know each other through and through. They've been friends ever since they were children, and this has been growing for years. They're genuinely deeply in love, and it's great to see them together. We didn't stand a chance, but they do. I think they'll be very happy together.'

'You don't think they should wait?'

'What for?'

Good question. She stared out of the window over the gently rippling waters of the loch and sighed. 'I don't know,' she murmured. 'To be more settled?'

'They are settled. Alec's got a good job—'

'One you've given him. Rob, you are sure about him, aren't you?' she asked, her anxiety surfacing. 'You don't think he's using her?'

Rob frowned. 'Using her? Of course he's not. They've known each other for years!'

'That wouldn't stop some people.'

'Maisie, Alec's not like that.'

'So what is he like? Tell me—I'm worried, Rob.'

'You don't need to be. They've known each other since they were children—he taught her to ride a bike, for heaven's sake. They used to play together when she came up in the holidays, and they've always got on. He was born in the cottage his parents still live in, and his father was my estate manager until he retired five years ago. He worked for my father, and my uncle before him, and his father before him, so he's the third generation to look after Ardnashiel. It's in his blood, even more than it is in mine, and I can't think of a safer pair of hands either for the estate or for Jenni. He's kind and decent, honest as the day is long, and he really loves her. You honestly don't need to worry.'

She nodded slowly, reassured by his measured assessment of his future son-in-law. 'And your mother? How does she feel about him?'

'She likes him. She's very fond of him, actually.'

'Really? Even though he's one of the estate employees? I'm surprised she thinks he's good enough for her.'

His brows scrunched together in a frown. 'What makes you say that?'

'Well, they made it clear I wasn't good enough for you—or was that just my lack of morals?'

He gave a harsh sigh. 'You don't change, do you?' he said. 'You always were a little too quick to judge.'

'I wasn't judging her, she was judging me! That's unfair!'

'Is it?' he said softly, his eyes searching hers. 'You didn't give my father the benefit of the doubt, you rebuffed all my mother's offers of friendship and you walked off and left me. *That* was unfair.'

She opened her mouth to argue, thought better of it, here in this public place, and shut it again. She'd tell him another time—maybe—just what his mother's offers of friendship had consisted of. And as for his father, there was no doubt to give him the benefit of. He'd hated her, despised her, and he'd made sure she and everybody else had known it. And she hadn't left him, she'd left the castle, and he'd let her go, made no attempt to follow her, to find out what was wrong.

'This is neither the time nor place to go over all of this,' she said, equally quietly. 'And anyway, it's time we got on. I'd like to see Jenni now, she'll be wondering where we are.'

And without waiting to see what he did, she got to her feet and walked out of the café, leaving her coffee half-drunk and her pastry in shreds all over the table.

Stifling a sigh, Rob threw down a few coins for the tip and followed her out, wondering how on earth they were going to get through all the inevitable meetings and discussions and tantrums that would eventually culminate in the wedding.

Ten and a half weeks, he told himself as he unlocked the car and held the door for her, and it would all be over and she'd be gone, and everything would get back to normal.

For some reason, that didn't feel comforting…

The road to Ardnashiel was painfully familiar to Maisie, and they travelled it in a tense and brittle silence.

The first time she'd driven it with Rob all those years ago, it had felt very different. They'd been laughing and holding hands as he drove, their fingers linked on his thigh, and he'd been telling her all about it, about the huge, sprawling estate his father had inherited ten years before from an uncle.

He loved it, he'd told her. He'd loved it as a child, coming up with his parents to visit his widowed uncle, not realising at first that one day it would be his, and he was looking forward to showing it to her. 'Since it's going to be mine. Not for years and years, though,' he'd added, laughing. 'I'm not ready to bury myself up here in the wilderness yet, by a long way, but one day, I suppose, the time will come.'

That day had come sooner than he'd imagined, when his father had died in a shooting accident eight years ago and he'd left London and moved up here for good. She'd never been back, though, not since the day she'd left and vowed never to return.

The road hadn't changed at all since then, she

thought, taking it in as her heart knotted ever tighter in her chest. A quiet, winding road that ran between lush green fields with fat cattle grazing contentedly. It was calm, bucolic, and it should have been beautiful, but it was coloured by association. The last time she'd travelled it, she'd been in a taxi, leaving it behind, and part of her was still the lonely, desperate young woman that she had been then.

He reached a junction and turned onto a narrow switchback of a road that clung in the gap between the edge of a loch and the wall of rock where the land met the water. It was an appalling road, and yet the fact that it existed at all in such a tight space was a miracle of engineering in itself.

The loch turned into a river, then the road widened as the land levelled out into a flat bowl around the harbour mouth, houses clustered along its walls, fringing the sea and running up towards the hills, and then beyond the small community, set up on its own on a rocky outcrop above the beach, was Ardnashiel Castle.

Built of stone, grey and forbidding, even with the sun shining on it there was a look of menace about it that chilled Maisie to the bone.

Just as it was meant to, really, since it had been built as a fort, but an ancestor had extended it two hundred years ago, creating a more civilised living area and carving gardens out of the woodland that had encroached on it. He'd added little turrets with tops like witches' hats, and made the windows bigger, and the first time she'd seen it she'd thought it was straight out of a fairy-tale, but then things had changed. It had ceased to be a safe haven and begun to feel like a prison, and looking at it now brought the feelings of suffocation crashing back.

And maybe Rob realised it because, as they crossed the stone bridge and drew up in the stable-yard by the coach-house, he glanced across at her for the first time since they'd left the café and sighed.

'I'm sorry,' he said quietly. 'I realise it's not your fault you don't know Alec, but give him a chance. Please. And my mother. I know you didn't always see eye to eye, but she's worried about seeing you again, worried you'll still dislike her.'

'I didn't dislike her, Rob,' she corrected him quietly. 'She disliked me. And I'm sorry if you felt I was being unfair to Alec. I will give him a chance, of course I will. I've always liked what I've seen of him, but—I'm just worried for Jenni, Rob. She's my little girl, and I'd hate to see her make a mistake.'

'It's not a mistake—and she's my little girl too, remember,' he said with a twisted smile that cut her to the heart. 'Just because she lived with you doesn't mean I didn't love her every bit as much as you did. And I know you feel I've stolen her from you, but she feels at home here.'

She opened her mouth to argue, to say of course she didn't feel that, she knew he hadn't stolen her, but then shut it again, because she did feel like that, did feel that he'd stolen not only her daughter but also her wedding, all the planning and girly excitement she'd seen so often in other young brides and their mothers, the tears and the tantrums and the laughter.

Which was ridiculous, because she was here now, for exactly that, and she would be here for as long as her daughter needed her.

'Rob, it's fine. Let's just move on, can we?' she said, and then the car door was snatched from her hand and Jenni was hurling herself into the car and hugging her, sitting on the sill and cupping her face, staring at her searchingly.

'Are you all right? I know you didn't want to come, but—'

'I'm fine,' she said softly, and gathering Jenni into her arms she hugged her hard. 'It's fine. And it's going to be loads of fun. Come on, let's go inside and we can start planning!'

'Brilliant, I can't wait. Here, look, my ring!'

She held her hand out, eyes sparkling, face alight with love and happiness, and Maisie looked at the ring, a simple diamond in a white gold band, nothing flashy but perfectly suited to her uncomplicated and slender daughter, and she smiled.

'It's lovely. Did he choose it?'

She giggled mischievously. 'I might have hinted a little,' she confessed, and Rob snorted.

'Only slightly,' he said. He was out of the car, taking her bags out of the boot by the time she'd disentangled herself from their daughter and climbed out, and she scraped her windswept hair back out of her eyes and reached for her camera.

Rob was there first. 'I've got it. You go on in with Jenni, I'll put this lot in your room.'

And she was led inside, Jenni's arm round her waist, and it was only as they went in that she realised things had changed.

The house was warm, for a start. Warm and bright and welcoming. It had never felt like that, not even in the summer, the year she'd had Jenni. And Jenni had taken her in through the front door, instead of round the side and in through the kitchen, the way Rob had always taken her in.

Through the tradesmen's entrance?

She was being ridiculous. He'd treated her as a member of the family instead of a visitor, but Jenni—Jenni was treating her as if she was special, a treasured and valued guest, ushering her in, smiling and laughing and hugging her, and as she led her into the drawing room, so familiar and yet so different, Helen Mackenzie got to her feet and came towards them. Older, stiffer, but still beautiful, still the elegant, dignified and aloof woman she'd always been.

'Maisie—welcome back,' she said softly, and held out her hand.

Maisie shook it, glad she hadn't kissed her or embraced her. It would have felt wrong after all the bitterness of the past, and the formal, impersonal contact was enough for now. More than enough. She found a smile and wished she wasn't wearing jeans and had had time to drag a brush through her hair.

'Thank you, Mrs Mackenzie,' she said politely, and then foundered, but it didn't matter.

Rob's mother simply smiled, said, 'Please, call me Helen,' and took up where she'd left off and asked if she'd had a good journey, and if she'd like a drink.

'Tea? Coffee? Or something cold, perhaps?'

'Actually, I'd love a glass of water.'

'Of course. I always get very dehydrated when I'm travelling. There just don't seem to be the opportunities to drink anything civilised. Jenni, my dear, would you ask Mrs McCrae if she could find us a bottle of spring water? Still or sparkling?'

'Sparkling would be lovely. Thank you.'

How stilted. How formal and civilised and polite,

when all Maisie wanted to do was head off with Jenni and hug her and hear all about Alec's proposal.

'Maisie, do sit down. You must be exhausted. I don't suppose you slept a wink on that wretched train. I know I never do.'

'It was very comfortable.'

'But not restful. It's not the same as a decent bed.' She looked down at her hands, flexing her fingers slightly, then met Maisie's eyes again, her own, so like Rob's and Jenni's, troubled. 'I'm glad you've come,' she said frankly. 'I did wonder if you would, but for Jenni's sake, if not for anyone else's, I think we should try and put the past behind us and move on—let bygones be bygones.'

She opened her mouth to speak, found no words that she was prepared to say out loud, and then was saved from answering by Jenni coming back into the room with Alec.

She got up to greet him and found herself wrapped in a warm, firm hug. 'Hi. I'm sorry I wasn't here to greet you when you arrived, I was just welcoming a group of guests, but I saw you drive by and gave them some flannel about checking on the nesting golden eagles and left them to settle in.'

His eyes sparkled mischievously, and Helen gave a rusty chuckle. 'You're a terror, Alec Cooper. Will you stay and join us for a drink, or do you have to be somewhere?'

'Checking the nesting eagles, for instance?' Maisie teased, and he laughed.

'No, I don't have to be anywhere. The guests have all been before, so they know their way around. They're all heading off to the pub for lunch, and I'm free for a while.' He took her hand in both of his, his eyes serious. 'So, will you forgive me? I'm sorry I didn't manage to talk to you, too. I did try, but your mobile must have been off, and I didn't leave a message. It didn't seem to be the sort of thing I could say to a machine, but—well, I know you've had reservations about me, and I really wanted your blessing, too…'

'Oh, Alec, of course I forgive you,' she said, guilt washing over her. He *had* tried to ring—the missed call from a number she hadn't recognised. 'And it's not that I have reservations, Alec. I don't really know you, and I just want you both to be sure, but Jenni knows you much better than I do, and you probably know *her* better than I do, come to that, so I have to trust your judgement. I just want my daughter to be happy, and she does seem to be, so of course you have my blessing. But look after her, Alec, treat her right. That's all I ask.'

'Of course I will. I love her, Maisie. I love her more than anything or anyone in the world. I'll do nothing to hurt her.'

Maisie's eyes filled, and she hugged her soon-to-be son-in-law hard, then reached out for Jenni, drawing her into the hug as well. Please let it be all right, she prayed, and then let them go, just as Mrs McCrae came in, set down the tray and engulfed her in yet another hug.

'Good heavens, lass, let me look at you. You don't look a day older! Oh, it's good to see you again.'

She laughed, delighted to see the kindly housekeeper who had been her saviour and only friend in the dark days after Jenni's birth. 'Oh, Mrs McCrae, how lovely to see you again, too! You haven't changed, either. I would have known you anywhere!'

'A few pounds heavier, mind, but my grandchildren keep me fit now when I'm not here running up and down stairs after this lot!'

She heard a door open and close, then Rob came in. 'Sorry to be so long. I was held up by a guest—something about nesting golden eagles?'

Alec chuckled. 'Ah—a little poetic licence. I wanted to greet my future mother-in-law, but it's not a problem. I'll tell them they can't be disturbed, and, anyway, we have got nesting eagles.'

'Have we?'

'Aye. I saw them this morning when I was out on the hills checking the deer. We've a stag needs culling, by the way. He's been injured—can't put one hind leg to the ground. It's the big old stag with the broken antler and the scar on his rump.'

Rob nodded. 'I wondered about him. He was lame yesterday, I was going to check on him. Can I leave him to you?'

'Sure.'

That dealt with, Rob turned to Maisie, scanning her face for any clue as to her mood, but she was smiling and talking to Mrs McCrae about her grandchildren and giving his mother a wide berth.

Oh, hell, it was all so complicated, he thought, feeling twenty-two again. If only she'd stayed, if only he'd tried to convince her to come back instead of letting her go without a fight. Or gone with her. They hadn't needed to live up here, they could have lived in London or Cambridge—anywhere, really, that she chose, but she'd chosen to leave him, to take his daughter away, and deny his parents the chance to see their beloved little granddaughter grow up. She'd even done it behind his back, while he'd been at sea, and asked his parents to tell him and give him her letter—a letter that had told him what he'd already known, that she didn't want to stay. She hadn't even had the guts to do it to his face. That, more than anything, had hurt.

He checked the thought and turned to his mother, concentrating on the practicalities. 'So— what time are we aiming to have lunch?'

'Whenever we're ready. Mrs McCrae, how long will lunch take to prepare?'

'It's all ready, Mrs Mackenzie, you just tell me when you want to eat. The bread's fresh out of the oven and I just need a few moments to heat the soup.'

'Ten minutes, then?' Helen said, and Rob wasn't sure if he'd imagined it, or if it was desperation that flickered briefly on her face before Maisie masked it.

'I think,' he cut in smoothly before anyone could argue, 'that Maisie could probably do with a few minutes to freshen up. She's been travelling all night. An hour, maybe?'

He hadn't imagined it. Her eyes met his with relief, and she gave him a grateful smile.

'Thank you. That would be wonderful—if you don't mind, Mrs McCrae? I don't want to put you to any trouble.'

'Och, of course I don't mind! I made cock-a-leekie for you, hen,' she said, beaming at Maisie. 'I know it's your favourite soup, and there's home-made oat bread, and some wonderful Mull Cheddar to follow. You always liked the Mull Cheddar.'

Maisie's face softened, and she smiled warmly at the elderly housekeeper. 'Thank you. That sounds lovely. Fancy you remembering I like cock-a-leekie.'

'I've never forgotten you, pet. I'm making roast beef for you tonight, for Alec's parents coming up. Just to welcome you home.'

She bustled off, and for a moment there was silence while the word 'home' seemed to reverberate around the room, but Rob cut it off swiftly.

'I'll show you to your room,' he said, and opening the door he ushered her out and closed it softly behind them.

'Thank you,' she said. That was all, but it spoke volumes, and he dredged up a smile.

'My pleasure,' he told her, wishing that it wasn't a lie, that every interaction between them, no matter how brief or businesslike, didn't seem to be flaying him alive. 'I've put you in the room you had before. You always used to sit there in the window and look out at the sea. I thought you might like it.'

Maisie felt a chill run over her. She'd wept so many tears in that room, and it was on the tip of her tongue to ask for another, any one, it didn't matter which, just not *that* room, but then she stopped herself and nodded. She had to get over this silliness. They had a wedding to plan, and she couldn't allow herself to keep harking back to the past.

'Thank you,' she said, and followed him up the magnificent old stone staircase to the landing above. He fell into step beside her, hanging back as they reached the room, and she wondered if he could hear her heart pounding with dread.

The door was standing open, and she went in and stopped in her tracks.

It was different. Lovely. The colours were soft and tranquil, muted blues and greens, pale cream, a touch of rose here and there to lift it. A great black iron bed was heaped with pillows and cushions and dressed with a pretty tartan throw so soft she wanted to bury her face in it and sigh with delight.

When had it been changed? And why? Not for her, of course. It would be a favourite guest room, with that gorgeous view out over the sea to the islands, and she realised in surprise it now had its own bathroom off it, in the little room that had been Jenni's nursery.

Progress, she thought in astonishment.

'It looks…'

'Different?' he murmured, and she turned and met his eyes.

'Yes.' Very different from the room she'd been installed in after Jenni had been born. That had been cold and forbidding, but this…

She ran her hand over the throw, fingering its softness. 'This is lovely.'

'It's a pastel version of the Mackenzie tartan,' he told her. 'Jenni's idea. There's one in every room—mohair, to keep out the cold.'

'It's warm in here, though.'

'Well, it is April. The heating works better now, but the wind still sneaks in in January.'

His smile was fleeting, and made her heart ache. She'd loved him so much...

'And an en suite bathroom. That's a bit luxurious,' she said, turning away as if to study it, just to get away from those piercing eyes.

'It *was* twenty years ago, Maisie,' he reminded her gently, as if she needed reminding. 'Things have changed. All sorts of things.'

Him? She said nothing, and after a moment she heard a quiet sigh. 'I'll see you downstairs. Come and find me when you're done—I'll be in my study.'

'Where is it?'

'Bottom of the stairs, turn left, follow the corridor round and it's at the back, by the gun court. Just yell, I'll find you.'

He went out, leaving her alone, and she closed her eyes and thought longingly of the bed. It looked so inviting. So soft and warm and welcoming. And she was shattered.

Later, she told herself. Shower first, then lunch, then talk to Jenni—and maybe later, before dinner, she'd snatch five minutes.

Anyway, her luggage was on the bed, waiting, and she'd have to deal with it before she could lie down.

'Shower,' she told herself sternly, and unzipping

her case she pulled out her wash bag and headed for the bathroom.

She didn't dawdle. Lunch was calling her, and she was more than ready for it by the time she'd tamed her hair, pulled on some clean clothes and tracked Rob down in his study overlooking the sea.

He was deep in thought, staring out of the window, feet propped up on his desk and his brow furrowed when she went in. He dropped his feet to the floor and swung round, greeting her with a smile that didn't reach his eyes. 'Everything all right?'

'Lovely, thank you. Much better,' she said with real gratitude, and he got to his feet and ushered her through to the drawing room where his mother, Jenni and Alec were waiting.

He'd gone into the study deliberately, she realised then, to wait for her so she didn't have to come in here alone and face them all. She could have laughed at that. If only he'd realised that he, of all of them, was the biggest stumbling block.

'I'll tell Mrs McCrae we're all ready,' he said, and left her with Jenni, striding down the corridor away from the scent of soap and shampoo and something else he recognised from long ago. Something that dragged him right back to the beginning, to the times when she would come to him smelling like that and he'd take her in his arms and hold her close and breath in the scent of her…

He went down to the kitchen, wishing he could escape, go out onto the hills where the fresh air could drive the scent from his nostrils and bring him peace. But he couldn't, because he had things to do, things that only he could do. His daughter was getting married, and he had to hold it together until then. And dragging Maisie into his arms and breathing her in wasn't an option, either.

'We're all here now,' he said to Mrs McCrae. 'Can I give you a hand?'

'Aye, that would be kind, Robert. You can stir this while I put the bread out.' And having trapped him so easily, in a trap he'd walked into with his eyes wide open, she then started on him in her oh, so unsubtle way.

'She's looking tired.'

'She is tired. She's been travelling all night. She looks better now she's had a shower and changed into fresh clothes.'

'She'd look better still if she'd come home and let me feed her up a bit,' she said, wielding the bread knife like a weapon. 'Poor wee thing.'

'I'm sure Maisie's perfectly capable of feeding herself,' he said firmly, drawing the pot off the heat and closing the lid of the range. 'And she has a home in Cambridge,' he added, reminding himself as much as Mrs McCrae as he glanced at the bare table. He frowned. 'Where are we eating?'

'In the dining room,' she said, her eyes flashing with indignation. 'Robbie, she's come back, wherever you say her home might be! She can't be eating in the kitchen—not today.'

He opened his mouth to argue, shut it again and sighed softly in resignation. 'I'll carry this,' he said, and followed her up the stairs.

'Here we are, hen,' she said, setting the bread down on the table as Maisie sat down. 'And mind you eat plenty!'

She did. She was still starving, the half-eaten pastry just a memory now, and she had two bowls of the delicious hearty soup, a good chunk of cheese and two slices of the soft, warm oat bread that was Mrs McCrae's forte. And while she ate, Jenni took the opportunity to fill her in on the wedding plans to date.

'OK. I've had a few ideas,' she said, making Alec splutter into his soup, which earned him a loving swat from his fiancée. 'You're not here for long, Mum, so I thought we should spend today planning and having a brainstorming session, and then tomorrow we're going to Glasgow to look at dresses. I've made some appointments, and I've made sure they know that there's only two months, but the places we're going all have samples which they can sell us, so we won't have to go through the business of ordering them, which takes ages. Now, they'll probably need altering, so…'

Rob watched her in wry amusement. She'd been planning this for ages, he knew, and Alec's proposal had been like a breath on a hair trigger. He just hoped that Maisie was ready for it.

CHAPTER THREE

'SHE'S amazing. Is there anything she hasn't thought of? She's so organised—it's like a military operation!'

Rob leant back against the ancient stone wall of the gun court, propped his elbows on it and chuckled, to her surprise. 'Did you really expect anything else?'

Maisie shrugged, turning to stare out over the sea below. 'I don't know. I hadn't really thought about it, but it never occurred to me she'd have it all down pat. What if it doesn't work out? What if something can't fit into her carefully orchestrated plan?'

'Then she'll have a little fit and learn the meaning of the word compromise,' he said drily.

Maisie shook her head. 'She's got all these ideas so firmly fixed. How long's she been planning it?'

His broad shoulders lifted in a casual shrug.

'Months? Years, probably. Come on, ever since she knew the meaning of the word bride she's been looking forward to this day. She just wants to be a princess. That's why Alec didn't ask her ages ago, he told me. He knew the second he said anything, she'd be off like a rat out of a trap, and so he had to wait until the time was right.'

'But—two months?' She winced just thinking about it, about all the plans that had to be put into action before the big day, but Rob seemed unperturbed.

'She doesn't need more than that, and he realised that if she had longer, she'd drive herself and everyone else round the bend. You know what she's like. Single-minded, determined, knows what she wants and gets it. Now, who does that remind you of?' he added drily, one brow arched in a mocking salute.

What? He thought she was like that? She nearly laughed out loud, because the one thing—the *only* thing—she'd ever really wanted was standing right there with her now, and she'd failed, lost the only thing she'd really, truly needed in her life.

The love of the man she adored, the man who had given her his child and then turned his back on her when she'd needed him the most.

'I think you overestimate my powers,' she murmured wryly.

'Well, let's hope not, because this wedding is all down to you now. I'll do what I can, but I'm up to my eyes with the estate and the summer's a nightmare with all the guests, so I can't tell you how glad I am that you're here to do it all.'

'But—Rob, I have a life, six hundred miles away! I can't just be here and sort it! I have things to do!'

'Can't you work round them? You can go back for the weddings—heaven knows there can't be that many, and your features you can write from here. You could do one on being a wedding planner.'

'What, and get tax relief on the wedding as a research tool, I suppose?'

'Well, it's a thought,' he said, his lips quirking. It drew her attention to them, to the clean, sculpted line of the top lip, the firm fullness of the lower. He'd kissed her with those lips, trailed them over her skin, driven her crazy with need with just the lightest touch—

Don't go there! Keep focused on the wedding.

She stroked her fingers over the barrel of an ancient cannon, testing the rough surface with her fingertips, searching for compromise. 'I have commitments, Rob. I can't just walk away from my life at a moment's notice.'

'So you'll need to commute. Go back for your weddings, if you've got commitments, and be here when you can. It's not for long.'

'It'll cost a fortune!' she said, horrified, but he just shrugged.

'So? She's your daughter. I'll pay your train fares. Talking of which, you'll need money for tomorrow. I'll give you a card and my pin number so you've got plenty of cash.'

'That won't be necessary. I'm buying her dress.'

'Ah. I wasn't thinking of the dress, I was talking about the train fare and incidentals, but…um…there might be a problem with the dress.'

She tilted her head, searching his eyes. 'A problem?' she echoed, a sinking feeling in the pit of her stomach.

'My mother wants to buy it for her.'

She felt herself recoil. 'No! I'm sorry, Rob. You can do everything else your way, but this is for me to do. She's my daughter. I'm buying her wedding dress. Tell your mother to give her something else.'

He sighed. 'She won't like it.'

'Tough. Sorry, Rob. I'm not backing down on this one, it means a lot to me,' she said implacably, meeting his eyes without flinching.

He studied her face for a moment, then nodded. 'All right. I'll tell her.'

And no doubt it would cause another rift—as if it would show, with something on the lines of the Grand Canyon already yawning between her and the woman who had been her mother-in-law.

'So—we're going to Glasgow tomorrow, is that right?'

'I believe that's the plan. You can park at the station at Fort William—'

'Aren't you coming?'

He smiled at her and shook his head slowly, his eyes laughing. 'Now, Maisie, surely you can work that one out. A girly day in town choosing wedding dresses and mother-of-the-bride outfits? Does that really sound like me?'

Oh, lord. She felt a moment of panic. 'I don't— Rob, talk to me about this wedding. I don't know anything about it, who's coming, how formal it will be, how dressy—anything. And I don't want to let Jenni down or look ridiculously overdressed, but I have no idea what's expected.'

'Just be there for your daughter, wearing whatever makes you feel good, so long as it doesn't clash with the bridesmaids or the kilts.'

'You're wearing a kilt?'

He smiled patiently. 'Of course I am, Maisie. I'm the Laird. All the men will be in kilts, particularly the groom's party. I'll be in the Mackenzie dress tartan, which is mostly green and blue with broad checks of white and a fine red line, and the Cooper tartan's green and blue but with a mauve line, so I think Jenni's working that in for the bridesmaids and Alec's cravat. The jackets will all be black. As for the day—well, that's a bit more complicated. There will be people who have to be invited, people who will expect to come as well as family and friends. And the villagers will expect it to be done right. My daughter's getting married. It's not often there's a wedding in the castle, so there'll be one hell of a party, make no mistake.'

'And you, I take it, will be footing the bill for this party?'

He chuckled wryly. 'Of course. We'll host a ceilidh for everyone in the evening. The marquee will be outside, and we'll just have to hope it doesn't rain, but if it does, these folk are Scottish, they're used to a bit of mist.'

She laughed at that. 'I seem to remember rather more than mist.'

His mouth tipped in a smile, but then the smile faded and he searched her eyes. 'You never did like the rain, did you? Or much else, come to that. Jenni asked me to be kind to you—she said you hated it here, that you'd be nervous about coming back.'

Oh, Jenni was right, she had certainly hated it here, especially at the end, but nervous?

'No. I'm not nervous. Concerned, perhaps. It wasn't a happy time for me.'

His jaw worked briefly. 'No. She said you'd be unsure of your welcome, but I hope you're not. You are welcome here, you do know that, don't you? Mrs McCrae's talked about nothing else since Jenni told her you were coming.'

'And your mother?'

She waited, holding her breath in the heartbeat of silence that followed, then he sighed and turned his head to stare out over the sea.

'She's not sure of her place. She's been mistress of the house for thirty-odd years, ever since my uncle died, and she's been unhappy here for most of that time. It's only since Jenni's been coming here regularly that she's seemed more settled, but now, with Jenni marrying Alec and moving out of the house, she's back to that strange limbo.'

'Because you're not married?' she asked shrewdly, and he nodded, his mouth twisting into a wry smile.

'Exactly so. She's mistress, and yet she's not. If I were to marry again, she'd be ousted from her place, and I think she's always wondered if that would happen.'

'Will it?' she asked a little rashly before her brain could control her mouth, but he just tipped his head slightly on one side and looked back at her with a curious, searching expression on his face.

'I don't know.'

'So—does that mean there might be someone? Am I going to have to share the top table with another woman at the wedding?'

He gave a startled laugh and shrugged away from the wall. 'No, Maisie. There's no other woman. I've only ever got close enough once and, frankly, that was enough in one lifetime.'

It should have reassured her, but it didn't. It unsettled her, as if by asking one question she'd prompted him to answer another, and the answer cut her to the quick. Suddenly he was standing too close, so close that she could feel his body radiating heat, reminding her of all she'd lost. She backed away.

'I'm tired,' she said. 'I might go and unpack, sort my things out a little before tomorrow, and the dogs look as if they're expecting you to take them for a walk. What time are we eating tonight?'

'Seven.'

'Fine. I'll see you at dinner. I'm looking forward to meeting Alec's parents. Actually, good point—do you still dress for it?'

He laughed and shook his head. 'No, we don't dress for dinner. We don't stand on ceremony much at all now, although Mrs McCrae still insists on serving us in the dining room. Usually we eat lunch in the kitchen, though. You were honoured.'

Honoured? She felt lost, dislocated from her life, from all the things that kept her sane.

'I'll see you at seven,' she said, and turning on her heel she crossed the lawn swiftly and went in through the door into the side passage, then up the back stairs to her room. She closed the door behind her with relief, then crossed to the window and sat on the padded seat where she'd spent so much time with Jenni as a baby, rocking her for comfort—but comfort for who? For the baby, or herself?

He was right, she thought, looking out of the window. The view was beautiful, and she'd always loved it, loved it for the freedom it brought her, the distance, the ever-changing landscape of the sea music to her soul. Rob was down there now, walking along the shore, heading up towards the ruins of the old castle.

They'd gone up there, sometimes, to be alone, that first September before she'd realised she was expecting Jenni, before it had all changed. It had been magical, their special place, almost sacred to them, but after they were married, of course, they hadn't needed to go there to be alone, and she'd missed it. Missed making love with Rob, the sweet scent of grass and the salt tang of the sea and the harsh cries of gulls all around them. They'd been such good times, infinitely precious. Where had they gone?

She rested her shoulders back against the shutters and let herself feel the warmth of the sun on her face. It was setting now, starting to fade as the evening wore on, and the sky was shot through with purple and gold.

She'd watched so many sunsets from this window in the days and weeks after Jenni's birth, counting the days to Rob's return, marking them off as the setting sun marked the end of each lonely and interminable day without him, and sometimes she'd taken Jenni and gone up to the old castle and stared out to sea, wondering where he was, desperate for him to come home. She'd been so lonely without him, but then, when he'd come back, there had been this strange awkwardness between them, a chasm she hadn't known how to cross, and she'd been even more lonely then.

The memory chilled her, and she rubbed her arms briskly and stood up, opening her case and shaking out her clothes. She'd only packed enough for a few days, but Rob seemed to think she'd need to be here for weeks.

We'll see, she thought.

Days were one thing. Weeks, she was beginning to realise, might be quite another…

'Rob tells me you want to pay for the dress.'

Maisie met Helen's eyes unflinchingly, not wanting to upset her but determined not to back down. 'Yes. I'm sorry, I know you offered, but I really feel it's my place.'

'Are you sure? Wedding dresses can be dreadfully

expensive, and I know you only work part time. I wouldn't want you to feel you had to scrimp.'

She hung onto her temper with difficulty. 'Helen, I can afford her dress,' she said firmly. 'And mine. Don't worry, she won't disgrace you—or, more importantly, herself. She can tell you all about it when we get back.' And then, because Helen's eyes were filled with hurt, she went on, her voice softening, 'If you really want to give her something to wear on the day, offer to pay for her veil. She'd be really pleased at that, and she can hand it on to her own daughter.'

As Maisie herself would have done, if she'd had the chance, but her wedding to Rob had been hasty, restricted to immediate members of the family, and under the circumstances the very idea of a veil would have been ludicrous.

She heard voices behind them, and Jenni clattered down the stairs, long auburn hair flying, eyes sparkling with excitement. 'Oh, this is going to be such fun. Are we all ready—? Oh, Grannie, why are you still in your dressing gown? Aren't you well?'

'I'm fine, but I've decided not to go with you, darling. This is for you and your mother to do. I'll look forward to hearing all about it when you get back.'

Had Helen been meant to come? Oh, no, she hadn't realised that, and for all Helen's faults, Jenni loved her grandmother. She felt a wash of guilt and turned to her. 'We can get a later train. Why don't you come—do what I suggested?' she said softly, but Helen shook her head.

'No. We'll get the veil some other time. You go together, you'll have a lovely day, and I get Jenni all the time now, don't forget.'

She hadn't. It was a constant ache that her darling daughter was so far away from her now, her life almost exclusively up here in the wilds of the West Highlands. And time spent with her was infinitely precious.

She nodded, touched at Helen's understanding, wondering if perhaps she had misunderstood her years ago, or if Helen had simply mellowed with age. 'Thank you. Come on, then, Jenni, let's go. We've got a lot to do.'

Glasgow was bustling, but the rain which had threatened earlier had cleared by the time they arrived and the sky was a glorious blue. Just as well, since Jenni had orchestrated a tight schedule.

They started at the top of her list and worked steadily downwards through the bridal shops and departments, and as she flicked through the rails of dresses, shaking her head, pulling a face, making 'hmm' noises, it began to dawn on Maisie what this task entailed.

Jenni tried on umpteen dresses in several shops,

standing on a box so that the dresses hung without crumpling on the floor, while the ladies adjusted them with huge clips at the back to pull them in if they were too big. Just so she could get the idea.

'How long would it take to alter them?' she asked again and again, and rejected several on the grounds that there simply wasn't time to have them taken in or up or both. Others were rejected because they were encrusted with crystals or smothered in embroidery or just didn't feel right, and in the end they couldn't remember what she *had* tried on. Lots, though.

They paused for coffee after the second shop, to catch their breath and sober up because in both shops they'd been offered sparkling wine, and then they tackled the third.

'That was awful. I hated everything in there,' Jenni said as they emerged, and they had a chuckle and found a café for lunch.

'Mummy, what are we going to do if I can't find anything I like?' she asked, picking her way through a toasted panini with a thoughtful look on her face.

'I don't know, darling. Keep looking?'

'I don't have time. And we've still got to get you sorted out.'

'Don't worry about me, I can get my outfit any time.'

'But I want to be *with* you! And I've got my

finals coming up, and if it's all going to be like this, it'll be impossible.'

She looked near to tears, and Maisie squeezed her hand. 'Darling, it'll be fine. I'm sure you'll find something. There are thousands of dresses out there.'

And none of them seemed to suit her, for one reason or another. It wasn't that she was being unreasonably picky, she just hadn't yet seen The One.

'Right, two more to go. Let's get on,' Jenni said, stuffing her list back into her bag and getting to her feet.

And then finally, when Maisie was beginning to think it would take at least another day, they went to the last shop on her list. It was down a side street, tucked away where you would scarcely find it even by accident, and they were led upstairs and ushered to a seating area by a kindly but efficient matron called Mrs Munro.

'What are you looking for? Grecian, retro, sixties, traditional, princess, vintage?'

'Something simple but interesting. I don't know. The feel of the fabric's really important, and I don't want a huge dress. Alec says if I look like a pavlova walking down the aisle, he's leaving.'

Maisie gave a splutter of shocked laughter. 'Oh, Jenni! I'm sure he didn't mean it.'

'I don't know about that.'

'He'll adore it, whatever you have,' Mrs Munro said sagely. 'If the dress is right for you, he'll only see you, my dear, believe me. Right. White, ivory, cream? Or a colour?'

'Not a colour. Ivory, probably.'

'And the wedding's quite soon, you say, so it has to be something in stock—so, will you be needing to allow a little extra room?' she asked with a twinkle, voicing the question that Maisie had been afraid to ask, but Jenni coloured and shook her head hastily.

'No, nothing like that. My fiancé works on a sporting estate. We have to fit round the seasons, and we didn't want a winter wedding and we didn't want to wait till next year.'

She nodded, made Jenni stand up and turn round, and then disappeared.

'Gosh, she's a bit scary, I can't believe she thought I was pregnant,' Jenni whispered, and Maisie suppressed a little flutter of panic.

'Let's just hope she knows what she's doing,' she whispered back, reining in her thoughts. 'I wonder what she'll come up with?'

Trumps. That was what she came up with. She emerged from a cluster of rails with a single dress and hung it on the rail by the door.

'Oh, look, Mum, it's gorgeous,' Jenni breathed. 'Look at the fabric!'

'None of them look anything on the hanger. That's why I don't encourage people to look at them like that, but I've never seen this one on, so let's try it and see.'

So Jenni disappeared into the fitting room, and Maisie sat and sipped spring water—not sparkling wine, because, as the scary matron said, one needed a clear head for these things and there'd be plenty of time for that later!

And then Jenni came out in a dress like nothing else she'd tried. It was exquisite, a beautiful off-white crinkled silk, with a strap over one shoulder and soft asymmetric pleats across the body, hugging her figure to mid-thigh and then flaring out in a flamenco-style skirt that swept the floor.

She looked—heavens, she looked like a bride, Maisie thought, filling up, and put her glass down hurriedly and pressed her fingers to her mouth.

'Oh, darling, you look…'

She couldn't finish, her eyes welling up and flooding over, and Jenni burst into tears and went into her arms.

'Oh, Mummy, I love it!'

'So do I. You look so beautiful—stand back, let me see you again. Turn round—oh, Jenni, it's fabulous.' She met the matron's eye and found an unexpected sheen in them.

Mrs Munro cleared her throat. 'That's the

dress,' she said firmly. 'I can always tell when I see it on. I wasn't going to show it to you, because I've only just had it in today and it could do with a wee steam, but I thought the moment I saw you it might be the one for you, and it is. Oh, it most definitely is.' And with a little sniff, she dished out tissues all round, gave Jenni a brisk hug and moved on.

'So the wedding's in mid-June, you say? We need to make sure this dress is ready for then. Now, I promise you I've only just had it in, and you're the first person to try it, so it really is a new dress, so you needn't worry about buying a sample that lots of people have tried on. And I must say, I don't think it needs any alteration at all. What height heel are you talking about?'

'Nothing huge. I haven't looked yet, but Alec's only three inches taller than me, so I don't want to tower over him.'

'Very wise. What size are you?'

She found a pair of shoes with the right sort of heel height that went beautifully with the dress, and when Jenni put them on the length was perfect.

'Oh, they're lovely. Are they for sale?'

'Indeed they are. So, all you need to do now is take your dress home, hang it up in a dark room with a cotton cover over it, and you'll be ready to go. It might need a wee steam just before the day, but we can see to that, if you like, and you can pick it up nearer the time. It's up to you. We just need to choose the veil, if you're having one, and then you're finished. So, where's the wedding? Somewhere windy?'

'Ardnashiel.'

The matron stopped and looked at her. 'Ah, you're *that* Jennifer Mackenzie,' she said, nodding in delight. 'I saw the announcement in the paper yesterday. Well, it could certainly be windy up there on the coast, but you couldn't want a more beautiful setting. A long veil can be a bit of a handful and it'll need anchoring firmly, but they can look wonderful in the photographs on a windy day. Have a look and see if there are any that take your eye.'

The veils were all beautiful, and caused more tears. 'I don't know what Grannie'll think if I choose it without her. She should be here—she's buying it for me,' she explained.

'You can always bring it back and change it,' Mrs Munro suggested.

'That's an idea, Jenni. Or you could bring her with you to choose it, and pick the dress up then. Maybe your father could bring you next week, on your way back to uni, and he could pick the dress up and bring it home.'

'That's a brilliant idea! And it would mean Grannie gets to help me and she'll feel involved, and we don't have to struggle with the dress on the train! Fantastic,' she bubbled, but Maisie hardly heard her, because echoing in her head were her own words.

He could bring the dress home. Not *take* it home, but bring it…

'So have you chosen your outfit yet?'

She dragged herself back from the brink and met the woman's eyes.

'Um—no. This has been sprung on me, really. I only knew about it three days ago.'

'So, do you have any thoughts?'

'Something pretty,' Jenni said, twirling again in front of the mirror and laughing in delight as the skirt swirled out. 'Not mumsy. She's not mumsy at all, she's a bit of a gypsy. She's practical and sensible and down to earth, and she needs something really beautiful to do her justice—and don't argue, Mum. I want you to look beautiful for my wedding, and it doesn't matter if you can't wear it again. But not one of those ridiculous mother-of-the-bride outfits. You're much too young for that.'

She smiled and shrugged, and the matron eyed her up and down. 'What colour are the maids wearing?'

'A soft lilac, I think,' Jenni told her. 'Alec's a Cooper, and the Cooper's got a mauve line. I wanted to pick it up.'

She nodded, and then eyed Maisie again and shook her head. 'You can't wear that colour. It would be awful with your colouring. You need something gentle—cream? That would be all right with the Mackenzie dress tartan the Laird'll be in. Jenni, do you mind if your mother wears cream?'

She stopped twirling in front of the mirror and turned round to face them. 'No. Why? Have you got something?'

'A lace dress—it's very pretty, very beautiful, actually, and it fits like a dream. I got it in for a mother of the bride but she changed her mind and decided to go for something more conventional on the knee. It's sleeveless, shorter at the front with a little fishtail skirt at the back just skimming the ankles, but it's got straps so you can wear a proper bra and it has a lovely little bolero with it. I'll get it.'

It was perfect. The moment Maisie put it on, she knew it was right. It hugged her figure, skimmed her hips and snuggled in under her bottom, and the bolero just completed the look.

'Wow, that's fabulous! Good grief! You look really hot,' Jenni said, and Maisie felt a soft tide of colour sweep her cheeks.

'Are you sure it's not too…?'

'Too *what*?' Jenni asked, and then shook her head and laughed. 'It's *gorgeous*, Mum! You look absolutely stunning. You'll blow Dad's socks off!'

She froze, her breath wedged in her throat, and then gave a strangled little laugh. 'I'm not sure that's a good idea,' she said, but Jenni just flapped her hand.

'Don't be silly. You look really beautiful. You have to have it.'

She did. She absolutely had to have it, even if she never dared to wear it, because nothing she'd put on in her life before had ever made her feel so good.

'I'll take it,' she said. 'I don't even want to know the price.'

'It's reduced, actually, because the lady had paid a non-returnable deposit, so I'm taking that off for you. Just take it as a sign.'

Sound advice. She decided to follow it, and just hoped there was enough space in her account for both it and the wedding dress. She paid for both, and the shoes, and then they said a grateful goodbye to the wonderful and really not so scary Mrs Munro and headed back towards the station.

'So, are we all done?'

'I think so,' Jenni said, and turned to her mother and hugged her. 'Thank you so much. I know Grannie wanted to buy me my dress, but I'm really glad you did. I wanted you to, so much.'

'And I wanted to. Never mind, we'll have to tell her all about it and she can see you in it next week when you choose the veil.'

'I've already chosen it, I think.'

Maisie smiled. 'But she doesn't know that, and

if you've got any sense, you'll make sure she doesn't, because I'm still feeling a little guilty.'

'Don't. We've had a fabulous day, and I love her to bits but you're my mother. It should be you. And I just adore your outfit.'

Maisie glanced down at the bag in her hand with a mixture of excitement and trepidation. What if Rob hated it? What if he thought it was inappropriate?

What if it blew his socks off?

'I adore it, too,' she admitted. 'What do you think about shoes? And do I need a hat? Or a fascinator?'

'Oh, they're fun.'

'I think they look as if a chicken's landed in your hair,' she said, and they laughed together, talking accessories over a shared pot of tea in a little café, and then, because neither of them had the energy to keep looking, they caught the next train home—there she went again, calling it home when it was no such thing—and arrived in time for supper.

'So, did you have a successful day?' Helen asked as she dished up Mrs McCrae's delicious cottage pie.

'Brilliant. I'll tell you all about it when Alec's not here,' Jenni said, wrinkling her nose at him mischievously.

'So this is it, then, is it? The One?' he asked.

'Mmm. It's gorgeous—absolutely huge, with a great puffy skirt and hoops and sleeves and—'

He tore a corner off his bread roll and threw it at her, and she giggled and ducked.

Dear heaven, she was still a little girl in so many ways, so full of fun and the boundless enthusiasm of youth. Maisie caught Rob's eyes and found an indulgent look in them she'd seen before, when Jenni was little.

They exchanged knowing smiles, and she felt her heart hitch in her chest. Oh, no. She was too vulnerable to him, and being forced into his company like this was leaving her wide open to hurt.

She wanted him so much—still, even after all this time, felt the same way about him as she had when she'd first met him—but she still didn't know him, couldn't trust him not to turn away from her again if things got sticky. She had to get away.

She looked down at her plate, playing with her food, trying not to think about him, because he was too dangerous for her.

'So I was thinking, as we've got the dress and my outfit sorted, I could go back to Cambridge early next week, perhaps Monday or Tuesday,' she said a little abruptly, and then listened to the echo of her words around the room.

There was a heartbeat of stunned silence, then

Rob said, 'But I thought we'd agreed you'd stay longer?'

She met his eyes again with forced calm. 'No. You suggested it, but if we can get the majority of the decisions made this weekend, there's no need for me to stay longer. A great deal of it can be done over the phone or the internet. So long as we've settled the guest list and ordered the invitations and the other stationery, I don't see any point in being here when Jenni's back at uni, and, besides, I have a lot to do at home.'

'She has a point, Dad—the important stuff's done, and she's got a life down there, you know. She can't just drop everything and be here to save you having to make a few phone calls.'

'Fine,' he said, a little curtly. 'Don't worry. I'm sure it'll be all right. I just thought—'

'Well, you thought wrong,' she said, quietly but firmly. 'I'm happy to come back if necessary, but I can't sit around here with my life on hold in case a decision needs to be made.'

'Apparently not. Well, you have to do what you have to do. Right, if you'll excuse me I'm needed—some guests want to plan their weekend's activities and I need to have a look at the website. There's a hitch.'

'It was working fine earlier,' Alec said, sounding puzzled, but Rob had pushed back his chair and was heading for the door as if he couldn't bear to be in the room with her another moment.

'Well, it's not now,' he said over his shoulder, and yanked the door open just as Mrs McCrae reached for the handle.

'Oh—are you away, Robert? I made sticky toffee pudding—'

'Save me some, I'll have it later,' he growled, striding away down the corridor and leaving them sitting there in a strained silence that nobody seemed to know how to break. Jenni got there first, reaching over and covering her hand, her eyes distressed.

'I'm sorry, Mum. I might have known it was too good to last,' she said after a moment, but Maisie just shrugged.

'Well, you didn't really expect it to be plain sailing, did you?' she said lightly. 'We were obviously going to disagree on something. We always did.'

Jenni nodded, and then smiled up at Mrs McCrae who was poised with the spoon and shaking her head after Robert. 'You're going to have to stop feeding me up, Mrs McCrae. I can't put any weight on, my dress fits perfectly.'

She smiled indulgently. 'Does it, hen? That's lovely. Just have a wee piece of the sticky toffee, then, to be on the safe side.'

'Give her a nice big chunk. I'll eat what she can't manage,' Alec said with a grin, and with his gentle charm he steered the conversation back into safer waters and Maisie felt herself relax again.

CHAPTER FOUR

SHE was going back.

Damn.

Not that he could work out why he wanted her here a moment longer. The whole time she was here he was restless and unsettled, and the last thing he needed was her announcing that she'd cleared her diary and could be here until the wedding, but he hadn't expected her to run away *quite* so fast. There was still so much to do, so many decisions to make, so much to sort out.

'Oh, dammit,' he muttered, flicking on the computer and scowling at the screen. There was nothing wrong with the website. Nothing at all. It was just an excuse to get away, like the guests who wanted to talk about their weekend activities. They'd already done that earlier, and Alec knew it full well.

So he wasn't surprised when there was a knock on the door a short while later, and Alec slipped through it and closed it softly behind him.

'Problem with the website, is there?'

He shoved the chair back from the desk and propped his feet up on the edge. 'Why's she going so damn soon, Alec? There's still tons to sort out. What have I done wrong?'

'Maybe she's just busy.'

'Bull,' he said shortly. 'It's just an excuse to get away. It's what she's always done when it gets too difficult—she runs away.'

'Well, you should know, you're the expert.' He shoved some papers out of the way and put a tray down on the desk. 'Here—I brought us coffee and some pudding.'

'More?'

He grinned. 'Always room for more. I'm going to have to get Mrs McCrae to teach Jenni how to make it.' He prodded the bowl towards him, and Rob picked it up and toyed with the sauce, dipping the spoon in it and trailing it over the top of the sponge.

'She just gets to me.'

'You don't say. Actually, I think it's mutual. I think the reason she's going is she's having trouble dealing with how she feels about you.'

'She doesn't feel anything about me. Well, that's not true. She hates me.'

'Does she?' Alec murmured. 'I wouldn't be so

sure. She doesn't look at you as if she hates you. Far from it.'

He frowned, prodding the pudding, releasing the gloriously warm, sweet scent of it, and then to stall a little longer he dug the spoon in and scooped up a chunk of sponge. 'I think you're wrong,' he said, pointing the loaded spoon at Alec. 'I think she's just antsy here. She's always hated it.'

'Why?'

He shrugged and put the spoon in his mouth, stalling again.

'She must have loved you once,' Alec persisted. 'Jenni says she's never known her to have a boyfriend.'

He stuck the spoon back in the bowl and dumped it on the table. 'Really?' he said, his voice flat as if the subject bored him, when the truth was he was riveted.

'Really. And she looks at you as if…'

'As if…?'

Alec shrugged diffidently. 'As if she's never really got over you. If you want my honest opinion, I think she still loves you.'

'Loves me?' He snorted and picked up the bowl again. 'Now I *know* you're talking rubbish. She'd got over me by the time she had Jenni. I wasn't here for the birth, and the next time I was home on leave, she could hardly bring herself to look at me. It went from bad to worse.'

'You were in the submarines, weren't you?'

'Yes—and away for months at a time with no contact. It wasn't exactly ideal, but I got such a chilly reception when I did come home that frankly I was glad to go back. She didn't get on with my father either, and she upset my mother all the time. Then when Jenni was six months old, I went back to sea again, and when I came home, she was gone.'

Alec scraped the last trace of sauce off his bowl and put it on the tray. 'Why?'

'I have no idea,' he said flatly. 'We never talked about it. She didn't even tell me to my face, just left a note for me, packed up all her things and took Jenni with her.'

'And you didn't go after her?'

He sounded incredulous, and Rob sighed shortly and rammed his hand through his hair. 'No, Alec, I didn't go after her.'

'Maybe that's where you went wrong?'

He snorted. 'I don't think so. Unlike some people, I can take a hint—and that was a hell of a hint. So forgive me if I think you're wrong about her. I think she was over me by the time I went away to the navy, and the only reason she didn't leave earlier was because Jenni was so small. She hated it here—hated the castle, hated the weather, hated my parents—it was a disaster. The only good thing to come out of it was our daughter, and she took her away from me. Frankly, if we can just get through the run-up to the wedding without killing each other, I think we'll be doing well.'

He met his future son-in-law's thoughtful eyes head on. 'So—was there anything else I can do for you, or are you just here to pick over the bones of my failed relationship with your future mother-in-law?'

Alec gave a huff of laughter and got to his feet. 'No, that was all. Finished with your coffee?'

He glanced at it. It was stone-cold, and it was the last thing he needed. He was wound up enough. 'Yeah, take it away, I'll get a fresh one when I've finished this. And, Alec? Look after Jenni. Make sure this didn't upset her.'

He nodded, picked up the tray and walked out, closing the door quietly behind him.

Rob sighed and dropped his head back against the chair, locking his hands behind his neck and staring at the ceiling. There was a water mark on it, and he made a mental note to check the plumbing in the bathroom above. Another thing to add to the endless list.

He checked his email, sorted out a glitch on the website—poetic justice, he thought drily—and then took the dogs out for a walk along the beach in the moonlight before heading back to the house.

There was a light on in Maisie's bedroom, and he could see her sitting there in the window, staring down at him. Watching him.

Was Alec right? Did Maisie still love him?

He felt his chest tighten at the thought, emotions he'd long put behind him crowding him. They'd walked together on this beach so many times at first, climbed up to the ruins to be alone together. They'd hidden a blanket up there in an old stone alcove, and when the weather was fair they'd stretch it out on the soft, sweet grass inside the ruined tower and make love for hours.

His eyes burned, his chest tight as he remembered the sweet moments they'd shared. She'd been a virgin when he'd met her, his the only hands to touch her. Such a precious gift, and he'd treasured it, but she'd taken it away from him when she'd left.

So long ago. Lifetimes.

Of course she didn't still love him. If she'd loved him, she would have stayed, but she'd walked away without a backward glance, and only a madman would have gone after her.

'Maybe that's where you went wrong?'

He glanced up again, frowning, but her light was off now. Was she still watching him in the dark?

Damn her. He didn't need this. His emotions

were like acid inside him, eating at him, and he felt more unsettled than he'd felt in years.

Whistling the dogs, he went back inside, poured himself a hefty malt from the distillery in the village, too restless to sleep, and tackled the sliding pile of paperwork on his desk.

'Mum?'

There was a quiet tap on the door, and Jenni put her head round.

'Oh, you're awake. Good. I've brought us tea.'

She pushed the door open and came in with a tray, setting it down on the table by the window seat and sitting next to Maisie. She put her arm out, and Jenni snuggled up, resting her head on her shoulder as she'd done for years.

'It's so nice, having you here,' she said. 'I miss you.'

'I miss you, too. We haven't had early morning tea together for ages.'

'I know—and it's all going to change when I marry Alec. We'd better make the best of it.'

'Mmm.' She rested her head against Jenni's, then asked the question that had been troubling her for days. Even Mrs Munro had raised the subject yesterday, and Jenni had blushed and denied it, but Maisie wasn't sure, and she wanted to be sure, because it simply wasn't a good enough reason for marriage. So cautiously, tentatively, she said, 'Jenni—you would tell me if you were pregnant, wouldn't you?'

Jenni lifted her head and stared at her mother for a second. 'Of course I would. Mum, I can't be pregnant.'

'There's no such word as can't,' Maisie said drily, but Jenni shook her head, a shy blush warming her pale cheeks.

'There is. I know I can't be,' she said softly, resting her head back down on Maisie's shoulder. 'I really can't. I told him ages ago that I wanted to be a virgin on my wedding night, so if he wanted to sleep with me, he'd have to marry me. And having decided to—well, we don't want to wait any longer. That's the only reason for the hurry. Nothing else, I promise.'

Maisie hugged her tenderly. 'Wow,' she murmured thoughtfully. 'That's novel. I wish I'd had half your sense.'

'I don't,' Jenni told her bluntly, 'or I wouldn't be here now, would I?'

'No, you wouldn't, and I wouldn't change that for anything,' she said, her hug tightening as she dropped a kiss on her daughter's hair. 'I'm just surprised.'

'Maybe all your lectures about respecting myself

and being sure about a relationship first have paid off. And I am sure. I'm really, really sure.'

'Good.'

Jenni sighed contentedly and shifted to look out of the window. 'He proposed to me up there, in the tower room of the old castle,' she said, her voice dreamy. 'It was so romantic. He took me up there, with a blanket and a picnic basket, and it was freezing, but he'd got hot pies from Mrs McCrae, and a flask of coffee, and when we'd eaten he got up, and I thought we were going, and I was actually relieved because it was so cold, but then he pulled me to my feet and went down on one knee and asked me to marry him. And I just burst into tears—isn't that silly?'

Maisie hugged her. 'Not silly at all.' It was what she would have done, if Rob had taken her up there and proposed to her like that, instead of telling her that they ought to get married when they hardly knew each other.

'I love the view from here, don't you?' Jenni murmured, and Maisie debated her answer and then avoided it.

'It's beautiful,' she said, because that was indisputable. 'I used to sit here with you for hours when you were a baby, staring out to sea and wondering where your father was.'

'It must have been very odd for you here

without him when he went off to the navy. You must have been so lonely without him.'

'I was. I didn't know anybody, and I didn't fit in. And I don't think they liked me.'

Jenni looked shocked. 'Why ever not? Did they think you didn't love him?'

'Oh, I loved him,' she said softly, 'but they knew nothing about me. We were so young, and we'd just met, and then what felt like minutes later he was off into the navy and I was pregnant. Classic timing. It was hardly a great start and not exactly what they'd planned for their only son.'

'But you did marry him, and you had me, and you still managed to do your degree. I think that's amazing.'

She gave a hollow laugh. 'Only in stages, and only because the college was very accommodating and let me take a year off in the middle. And I really struggled that first year, while I was pregnant and he was away so much.'

'Why *did* you move up here?'

She eased Jenni out of her arms and reached for her tea with a quiet sigh. 'I've often asked myself that. Maybe because I thought I'd get more support from them than I was getting from my own family, and maybe I hoped that if I came to love the castle he was so fond of, then our marriage would stand a chance. It didn't work like that, though. It was cold and wet, and I was trapped inside the castle with you for days on end. I couldn't drive then, and there was nowhere to go while he was at sea, and anyway most of the time it seemed to be raining. Then when he did come back he wanted to go out walking on the hills on his own, and I got resentful, and he was withdrawn, and we just stopped talking. Stopped everything, really. If we weren't talking about you, we didn't talk. We never spent any time together that wasn't with you or about you, and most of the time he wasn't here anyway, so what was the point of me being here with you when I felt so unwanted?

'So I took you back home with me, and he let me go. He didn't come after me, didn't ask why— nothing, not for months, and then it was just a letter from the solicitors. I think it was a relief to him. The trouble was, we were both just kids, and we behaved like kids, so it's no wonder it didn't work. Anyway, we got divorced as soon as we could, and I vowed never to come back.'

Jenni's eyes filled with tears. 'Oh, Mum, I'm so sorry. I didn't realise you were that unhappy here. I thought it was just the weather and Dad being away. I mean, I knew you didn't have much in common, but—it must have been awful. No wonder you left.'

She tried to smile, but there was a lump in her

throat she was having difficulty swallowing, so she just shrugged and drank her tea, and Jenni snuggled into her side again and said nothing for a while.

'We ought to sort out the guest list,' Maisie said in the end. 'Have you done anything about it?'

'Sort of. Dad and Grannie need to get together and talk about relatives and things, and you need to tell us who you want on it, but we've done ours, and Alec's asked his best man and ushers and I've contacted Libby and Tricia.'

'Is that all you're having as your bridesmaids?'

'Mmm. They need to come and look at dresses—we can do that in Glasgow one day. And we need to sort out the wedding invitation wording, and get them ordered, and I suppose we need to talk about flowers.'

'Have you had any ideas?'

'Mmm. I want white—just white, with lots of greenery. I think it looks beautiful. Really simple. Maybe white peonies. Apparently they smell gorgeous.'

'Yes, they do. They're lovely. And in mid-June that's perfect. What about table centres?'

'I don't know. Do you think I should have tall vases, or fishbowls, or low posies? There are so many styles and I'm just confused. Can you help me? You go to lots of weddings, you must have tons of ideas.'

'Do you want to look through my portfolio?' she suggested. 'I've got loads of weddings on there, and it might give you some ideas. In fact, the wedding I did on Wednesday was lovely. They had simple hand-ties for everything, and they looked fabulous. And that was just green and white.'

She turned on her laptop and brought up the photos of Annette's daughter's wedding, and they discussed the flowers, the bridesmaids, the favours, the table settings—everything except Annette. Maisie didn't want to add any more emotion into the mix, and some things weren't hers to talk about. She'd only told Rob because she'd ripped his head off when he'd pushed her buttons, and she'd wanted to get them off on a more even keel for this difficult visit.

Not that the uneasy truce had lasted long, she thought with a weary sigh, flicking through to another wedding, another set of options to consider.

'Oh! Mum, who's going to take the photos?' Jenni asked, looking suddenly concerned, but Maisie just hugged her.

'I thought we could ask Jeff. You know, from the paper? He's only young, but he's a good photographer and I can brief him thoroughly. Or we can get someone else?'

'No. No, I like Jeff. Oh, that's pretty,' she said, her attention distracted by another photograph, and they carried on looking through the file—until Maisie's stomach rumbled.

Then she realised what the time was. 'Jenni, it's after nine! We ought to get dressed and go downstairs and get your father and grandmother round the table, even if Alec can't be there.'

'He can. He's coming in for coffee at ten-thirty, and he's bringing Dad. And hopefully he'll stay and talk this time. I can't believe he walked out like that last night.'

'Oh, I can. It's his way, Jenni—or at least, his way with me. But I'll do my best to keep the peace, and hopefully he'll do the same, and we'll be able to get through it all in the next couple of days so I can go home for a while. I didn't even water the garden before I left, I was in such a rush, and I've planted up all my pots.'

'I'll miss you, you know,' Jenni said softly. 'I'm really enjoying having you here. It seems right, somehow.'

Did it? Not to Maisie. Not with Rob on a hair trigger and her stomach in knots because she knew she was falling in love with him all over again. But she'd miss her daughter, too. Unbearably.

'You're going back to uni, don't forget, so you wouldn't see me if I was here—and, anyway, I'll be back,' she said comfortingly, wondering how she'd cope with repeated visits but knowing she would have to in the future if she wanted to get to know her grandchildren.

'You'd better be back! I'm going to need you here before the wedding, Mum, making sure everything's in place. I really, really can't take my eye off the ball at this stage. I have to pass my finals or the last three years will have been wasted.'

'I'll be here,' she said firmly. 'Don't you worry about it, Jenni. I'll be here whenever necessary, and I'll do whatever I need to do to make your wedding day perfect.'

'So, that's the guest list finished, then? Mum, are you sure that's all you want to invite?'

'I'm sure,' she said, and Rob leant across the table to study the list upside down, and frowned at Maisie.

'Your father's not on there.'

She shrugged. 'He won't come. He thinks you're the spawn of the devil and we're well suited, in his words. There's no point in asking him, even if he was well enough to come, which he's not. I've tried and tried and tried to build bridges, and he sabotages every attempt I make, so I've given up.'

'Jenni? Would it make any difference if you asked him?'

His daughter shrugged. 'I never see him, Dad. It doesn't matter, really. He's so cold to Mum, and he ignores me whenever we see him at any family functions, and I don't know him. It's fine.'

'I still think he should be given the option.'

'OK, I'll ask him,' Maisie said shortly, 'but he won't come. He probably won't even reply.'

'And the rest of your family? Your brother and his wife and kids? Will they come?'

'They might. I don't know. It's a long way and he's very busy with school exams at this time of year. He might not be able to get away, but they're on the list.'

'So how many are there?'

'Not quite a hundred,' Jenni said, totting up quickly. 'So I expect by the time some people can't come because it's short notice, we'll be down to ninety or so.

'Which is fine. Alec and I have been looking, and we reckon we can seat a maxiumum of a hundred and twenty in the Great Hall, and it opens onto the side lawn where the marquee will go, so depending on the weather we can eat in or out and the catering tent can be situated so it's convenient for either. We can make a decision the day before, and we can have the reception drinks out on the gun court if the weather holds.'

'So how many invitations do we need to order?' Alec asked, making notes.

'Allow plenty in case of errors. And we need to

sort out the wording.' Rob met Maisie's eyes, knowing he was stepping straight into a minefield here. 'Any suggestions?'

'Well, Mr and Mrs Robert Mackenzie won't work,' she said with heavy irony. 'How pompous do you want to be?'

He felt himself frown. 'Pompous?'

'Yes—you know, "The Much Honoured Robert Mackenzie, Laird of Ardnashiel, and Ms Margaret Douglas request the pleasure of the company of— leave blank—at the marriage of their daughter Jennifer to Mr Alec Cooper in St Andrew's church, Ardnashiel, on Saturday 19 June at 2 p.m., and afterwards at Ardnashiel Castle. Carriages at Midnight, or whatever. RSVP to…", blah de blah— or do you think that sounds just a touch stuffy?'

One eyebrow was slightly raised, her mouth twitching, and her eyes flashed with challenge. Jenni was struggling not to laugh, and he took a slow breath.

'I think we could dispense with the "Much Honoured", don't you?' he said drily, refusing to allow her to needle him. He'd had a fairly pointed lecture from his daughter on the subject already that morning, and the last thing he needed was another one. 'How about "Robert Mackenzie and Maisie Douglas"—assuming you refuse to use your married name?'

'I do. I'm not married any more. I go by Douglas.'

'So "Robert Mackenzie and Maisie Douglas request the pleasure of your company at the marriage of their daughter Jennifer to Alec Cooper", et cetera, et cetera. I think that's pompous enough. What do you two think?'

'How about "Alec and Jenni would love you to join them for their wedding on" blah blah?' Jenni said, folding her arms and leaning back, her eyes every bit as challenging as her mother's, and he had to press his lips together to stop himself from laughing.

'Mother?'

'I think your version, Robert. It says enough and not too much. I think you could work "of Ardnashiel" into your name, though. You are the Laird, like it or not, and it'll be expected.'

'I agree,' said Maisie. 'We ought to write it down. I don't suppose anyone can remember what we said?'

How much more?

The guest list was finalised—at last—and they'd done the invitation format and discussed the inserts, such as map, directions and gift list, discussed the wording of the evening invitations, and then a thought occurred to her.

'I suppose the church is free on that day, before

we rush ahead and get the invitations printed?' she murmured, and there was a little nod from Jenni.

'It's free, I checked this morning. It's all sorted and booked, subject to him talking to us. Alec, we have to go and see him later, and he'll read the banns tomorrow. Mum, Dad, you'll both have to come. I really want you there, and Alec's parents. You'll be there, too won't you, Grannie? You always are.'

'I most certainly will, darling. As you said, I'm always there, every Sunday morning.'

Polishing her halo, Maisie thought, and then squashed the unkind thought. There was no room for her old resentments, and she had to try and let them go, for everyone's sake.

'Good. That's that sorted. Right, what else? Oh—flowers. I was looking at Mum's photos, and we've decided just white with greenery—'

She was interrupted by a soft gasp from Helen, and Maisie looked at her distressed face and her heart sank. Now what?

'Not green and white—please, Jenni. Something colourful, darling. It's a wedding.'

'But I don't want colourful. I want just white.'

'No—!' And without another word, Helen pushed back her chair and hurried from the room, her hand pressed to her mouth.

'What on earth's the matter with Grannie?' Jenni

asked, utterly confused. 'Whatever's wrong with green and white? It's not exactly controversial.'

'I don't know. I'll go and find out,' Rob said, and followed his mother out of the room. He came back a short time later, and sat down heavily.

'They were the colour of the flowers at my father's funeral,' he said softly. 'I'd forgotten. Can you bear to have something different?'

Jenni swallowed, shrugged and said, 'I suppose so. I'll have to, won't I? I can't upset Grannie,' and then she, too, left the room in tears, followed by Alec.

Maisie met Rob's eyes across the table.

'Are you going to burst into tears and rush off?' he asked, and she gave a low laugh.

'No, I think you're safe.'

'Thank God for that. Do you fancy a coffee?'

'We've just had one.'

He smiled conspiratorially. 'No, I mean a *real* coffee. With a wicked pastry and lots of froth and no overwrought emotions.'

She regarded him steadily, suppressing the chuckle in her throat. 'I can't promise that, but for the sake of the pastry, I'll give it my best shot.'

He grinned. 'That's my girl,' he said, and, standing up, he ushered her out of the door and round to the stableyard, grabbing a couple of jackets off the hook by the back door on the way out. He unlocked his car and folded down the roof while she pulled the fleecy jacket on, settled herself in the car and fastened her seat belt, then they set off, while she sat there and listened to his voice saying *'That's my girl'* over and over in her head.

CHAPTER FIVE

'So, what did you want to talk about?' she said, once they were seated with their coffee and pastries, and he arched a brow.

She couldn't quite hold in the smile. 'Let me guess—Jenni had a go at you and told you to apologise?' she asked, and he snorted quietly, his mouth quirking in a reluctant grin.

'Actually, Alec got there first. He had a go at me last night. And Jenni had a go this morning. But for what it's worth, I was going to apologise anyway. I didn't mean to walk out like that, but the thought of you bailing out on me and leaving me to cope with the tantrums was more than I could take, and this morning just underlined it all.'

'I'm not bailing out on you,' she said softly. 'But I do have things to do, as I told you before. I've got to sort the wedding photos for two weddings now, and get the albums ordered, and there's a rush job for the one I did on Wednesday because until Annette's had her chemo there are still question marks, so I absolutely can't let them down, and I've still got to do my regular column in the paper as well as other features. I can't just walk away from my commitments.'

He sighed and scrubbed a hand through his hair, making it stick up so her fingers itched to reach out and smooth it back down, to touch it, to sift it through her fingertips and see if it still felt as soft, as thick and rich as it had…

'No, I know you can't. I'm sorry if I implied you weren't taking the wedding seriously. Of course you've got a life down there, and I don't underestimate the importance of your work. I think you've done amazingly well, forging your twin careers while you've been bringing Jenni up, and of course you have to honour your commitments. I was just panicking.'

'You, panicking?' she teased. 'That doesn't sound like you.'

His smile was wry. 'My daughter's never had a wedding before.'

'Oh, well, at least we've only got the one—unless you've got any others stashed away somewhere that I don't know about?'

'Hardly. One's quite enough to worry about.' He sat back, stirring his coffee thoughtfully. 'So how are you getting on with Alec?'

Maisie smiled, feeling a little wave of affection for the decent young man her daughter had fallen in love with. 'Very well. You're right, he adores her.'

'He does.' He put the spoon down with exaggerated care. 'Do you know why the wedding's so rushed?'

'Jenni did tell me—when I asked her if she was pregnant.'

He chuckled softly, then his eyes locked with hers and his smile faded. 'I envy them. I envy them for being so sure, for having the time to learn how to love each other, for having the common sense to wait and do things properly. Maybe if we'd done that, things might have been different.'

'They would. We wouldn't have had Jenni, for a start, so I can't wish it undone, Rob. But I might wish it done better. Differently.'

'How?'

She sighed softly, fiddling with the crumbs on her plate, her hair falling forward and shielding her eyes from his searching gaze. 'Maybe if you hadn't gone away to the navy? If my father hadn't thrown me out?' She lifted her head and met his eyes. 'If your father hadn't thought I was a tramp?'

He went very still. 'Oh, come on, he never thought that.'

'Oh, he did. He said so. I heard him, talking to

your mother. You were away—it was just after I'd had Jenni.'

Emotions chased through his eyes, and she watched them, watched as the truth registered. He let out his breath on a quiet, slightly uneven sigh. 'I took you away from your familiar surroundings and brought you here because I thought you'd be happier here, better looked after, but it was a disaster, wasn't it?'

She nodded. 'They didn't want me. Why would they? My own family didn't, what on earth made either of us think yours would?'

He dropped his elbows back onto the table and steepled his fingers, pressing them thoughtfully against his mouth. 'Maisie, I'm so sorry,' he murmured. 'No wonder you left.'

'And you didn't follow me.'

'You didn't want me to.'

'Oh, I did, Rob,' she said softly. 'But you couldn't cope with it all, any more than I could.'

His eyes clouded. 'No, you're right. I couldn't. I was spending months at a time under the sea, desperate for the feel of the wind in my hair and the sun on my face, and when I was home you were sad and withdrawn, the baby was crying, and I didn't know what to do to help you.'

'Because you didn't know me. And I didn't know you, Rob,' she said softly. 'I didn't even know you were going to be a Laird until we came up here.'

'What's that got to do with anything? It's not as if I'm the clan chief. I'm just a squire, really. It's virtually meaningless—feudal nonsense.'

'No, it's not. It has implications for where you live your life. There's no choice, if you're going to do it properly. The Laird of Ardnashiel lives in the castle on the estate. End of.'

'It's not exactly Siberia,' he said defensively, but she just arched a brow.

'Really? It feels like it in the winter, believe me, when you can't drive and you're stuck there with a little baby and her father's out there somewhere under the sea out of reach for months at a time. And it doesn't help when his parents despise you and only tolerate your presence because you've got their grandchild.'

'I had to go to sea. You knew I was committed to the navy for six years.'

'But not the subs,' she said, feeling the old frustration and disappointment rise up. 'You could have switched—even if you'd been at sea, we would have been in touch then, I could have talked to you from time to time, but no. You *chose* to go into the submarines, you *chose* to isolate yourself from us for months at a time, and left me there alone.'

'You weren't alone!'

'Wasn't I?' she asked softly. 'Who was there for me, Robert? Not your parents, that's for sure. Your father thought I was a slut, and your mother thought I was a gold-digging little whore, deliberately getting pregnant to get my hands on the estate I didn't even know you had coming to you, though who knows why anyone in their right mind would want to live in a forbidding pile of rock somewhere just shy of the Arctic Circle? If it hadn't been for Mrs McCrae taking me under her wing, I seriously think I wouldn't have survived it.'

He stared at her, his face expressionless, and then he stood up. 'Come on, we're leaving,' he said, and walked out.

She heard his footsteps crossing the room, then someone coughed, breaking the silence, and the conversation resumed around her, a low hum, and speculative glances...

She followed him out, and found him standing down by the shore, hands rammed in his pockets.

He turned to her, his eyes searching.

'Was it really that bad, Maisie?'

She gave a choked laugh. 'Oh, yes, Robert, it really was that bad. And now they all know,' she added, gesturing to the café behind her.

He waved a hand dismissively. 'They're tourists. They don't know who we are, it doesn't matter.'

'So why didn't you stay and finish the conversation?'

'Good idea. You can tell me why you left me, and took my daughter with you.'

'You left me, Rob! You left me here, at the mercy of your parents. I felt utterly abandoned. Is it any wonder I walked away? And I didn't leave you, I left Ardnashiel. Maybe I should have stayed away and let sleeping dogs lie.'

He held her eyes for several seconds, then without another word he turned on his heel, strode back to the car and got in, staring straight ahead while he waited for her to join him.

Once again, the drive back to the castle was conducted in a screaming silence.

'Where did you go? We were looking for you everywhere, and then Alec spotted the car was missing.'

Rob put the roof up and got out without a word, leaving Maisie to talk to Jenni. His emotions were at fever pitch. He and Maisie needed time and space to talk, but of course there wasn't any, and there was probably no point in any case. It was all water under the bridge, over years ago, but he was deeply troubled by her description of her time there without him.

*If it hadn't been for Mrs McCrae taking me
under her wing, I seriously think I wouldn't have
survived it. You left me there. I felt utterly abandoned. I didn't leave you, I left Ardnashiel.*

'Where's your grandmother?' he said a little
shortly, and Jenni's eyes widened with distress.

'Have you two been fighting *again*?' she said,
and turning to Alec she threw herself into his arms
and sobbed.

'Damn,' he muttered, and strode off into the
castle, looking for his mother. He found her in the
drawing room, reading a book, of all things, while
the world went to pieces. He took it out of her
hand. 'Talk to me,' he demanded abruptly. 'I want
to know what went on here while I was at sea.'

She went very still. 'Robert, nothing went on.'

'That's not how Maisie sees it.'

'Well, that doesn't surprise me, she never did
make any attempt to see it from our point of view.'

'And what point of view was that?'

'Oh, come on. You were young, rich, poised on
the threshold of your life—you were a good catch,
Robert, and she caught you. Your father said she
was a tramp—'

'*Don't—ever—call her that again,*' he said, his
voice deadly quiet. 'Not that it's any of your damn
business, but Maisie was a virgin when I met her.
And besides, if she'd been after my inheritance,

don't you think she would have stuck around? She hasn't even taken maintenance from me all these years!'

She bristled. 'Why would she need maintenance? You gave her a house—the house we'd given you for your eighteenth birthday! What more could she want?'

'A home? A husband? Someone to love her—someone whose parents didn't think she was a gold-digging little whore? She heard you, Mum. She heard you and Dad talking.'

His mother went white, her eyes widening with distress. 'No! She wasn't meant to hear—'

'You're damn right she wasn't. You weren't meant to have said it! I trusted you to look after her, to keep her safe, to make her welcome, and all you did was regard her with disgust and suspicion.'

'But your father said—'

'I know what my father said, and I have no need to ever hear it again. That doesn't excuse you. I think you owe her an apology, and I think you should do it now, before she leaves.'

'She's leaving? So soon?'

He gave a short laugh. 'Give me one good reason—just one—why she should stay another minute!'

She couldn't. Of course not. There wasn't one.

He walked away, looking for the dogs, needing

to escape, and found them in the kitchen, sitting hopefully at Mrs McCrae's feet.

'Lunch is all ready when you are,' she said, and he stared at her blankly. Lunch? What did lunch have to do with anything?

'You'd better hold it,' he growled. 'I don't think there's a snowflake's chance in hell of us all sitting down together at a table right now. Dogs?'

'Oh, dear, no, no' another scrap, Robert,' she tutted, but he ignored her, slapped his leg for the dogs and went out. They dragged themselves away from Mrs McCrae and followed him along the shore and up to the ruins of the castle, and he stood there, in the broken remains of the tower where he and Maisie had spent so much time, waiting for his emotions to subside, for some semblance of peace to come.

It didn't.

But Maisie did, her footsteps almost silent on the soft grass, any noise drowned out by the whisper of the wind. The dogs alerted him, running to greet her, and he waited, turning towards her, arms folded, letting her set the tone.

'Can we talk?'

He gave a short laugh. 'I don't know—can we? We can't usually manage it but it's probably about time.' He looked down, scuffing the grass with his toe, then he looked up and met

her eyes again. 'I owe you an apology—again.
We all do.'

'I've seen your mother. Apparently she didn't
know I'd overheard those things, and she's mor-
tified.'

'Good. She needs to be. I'm so angry with her.'

'You upset her, Robert.'

He snorted. 'Not nearly as much as she upset
me, I can tell you.'

'I'm sorry.'

'What for?'

She shrugged. 'Causing a scene in the café?'

He laughed softly and held out his arms, the
fight going out of him. 'What a mess. Come here,
Maisie. You look as if you could do with a hug,
and I know I could.'

She hesitated, looked around at the place where
he'd held her so many times, and for the first time
in twenty years, she went back into his arms.

They closed around her, folding her firmly
against the solid warmth of his chest, and she
rested her head against his heart and listened to
its even, steady beat while the tension drained
out of her. Lord, how she'd missed this—missed
the feel of his arms, the strength of his body, the
sound of his heart under her ear.

They stood like that for an age, silent, un-
moving, just holding on, and then she lifted her

head and met his eyes, easing back a little but still standing in the loose circle of his arms.

'We should go back,' she said. 'Jenni's terribly upset. She hates rows at the best of times, and she's got her finals coming up, the wedding to organise—the last thing she needs is us coming to blows. We need to put this on one side and concentrate on her for now.'

'I agree. And the wedding's only the start of it, Maisie. OK, it might be a bit soon to start thinking about it, but—well, one day we're going to be grandparents. It might be an idea if we were at least friends. It's a pity you don't live closer.'

'I know, but my life's in Cambridge, Rob. And as you said yourself, it's not exactly Outer Mongolia up here.'

'Siberia.'

She felt herself smile reluctantly. 'Whatever. I can see Jenni and Alec and the grandchildren whenever I want. I can come and stay with them— presumably they'll be living on the estate?'

'Yes, they're moving into the gatehouse. It's pretty, it's got a safe, enclosed garden, it's the closest to the village for Jenni to socialise with other mums when the time comes, and it's ideal. It's got four bedrooms, so there'll be plenty of room for you, and there are always other cottages we can put you in if you'd rather. And ultimately, of course, they'll have the castle.'

'Not for a long while, I hope.'

His mouth quirked into a gentle smile. 'Hopefully not. And in the meantime, do you think we can try and be friends? Maybe get to know each other, at last?'

'Not before time.' She smiled up at him wryly. 'Did you know Alec brought Jenni up here for a picnic on Tuesday night and proposed to her?'

'Here? No, I didn't.' He gave a soft laugh. 'How ironic they should choose the place she might have been conceived.'

'I know. She said it was freezing, but very romantic.' She swallowed, trying not to think about the past, about lying with him under the stars on the blanket he'd hidden here, huddled together for warmth. They'd been cold, too, but it had been worth it, just to be alone with him away from prying eyes.

Until it had all gone wrong.

'I'm not surprised he planned it like that. He adores her—and he's picking up all the pieces at the moment,' he said with a sigh. 'I suppose we'd better go and pour oil on the troubled waters and let him off the hook.' He let her go, stepping back so she felt the chilly wind cooling her body where it had been in contact with his. It made her shiver, and she turned and headed back down to the castle, Rob behind her and the dogs running around their feet, while she wished—oh, how she wished—that things could have been different.

They walked in through the kitchen door to a welcoming committee of anxious faces and reddened eyes.

'So, Mrs McCrae, what's for lunch? I'm starving, and we've got a wedding to finish planning,' Rob said, and there was a collective sigh of relief as she bustled to the stove and pulled the stockpot onto the hob.

'A good rich broth to keep the wind out, and I found some more cheese yesterday at that café and shop on the way to Fort William. You know the one. It's new, Maisie. You might not have seen it, lass.'

Rob met Maisie's eyes and one brow hitched— a tiny movement only she would have noticed, she was sure, and she smiled wryly and looked away. 'I do know the one,' she said blandly, and pulled a chair out and smiled at everyone. 'Right, what else needs considering?' she asked, settling herself down at the scrubbed old table where she'd spent hours in that long-ago winter, keeping Jenni warm by the stove while Mrs McCrae had bustled around them.

'Tons,' Jenni said, looking despairing.

'What are you doing about the wedding cake, hen?' Mrs McCrae asked her, spoon poised over the pot. 'Because a good fruit can't be hurried, and you've only got ten weeks today. I'll need to be getting on wi' it.'

Jenni and Alec exchanged glances. 'Um, we don't really like fruit cake,' Jenni said carefully. 'In fact, lots of people don't like fruit cake. We thought we might not bother.'

Mrs McCrae turned to them, her face scandalised.

'Y'have tae have a cake!' she exclaimed in horror.

Oh, no, another fight brewing, Maisie thought, and chipped in.

'At some of the weddings I've been to, they've had a cake made of cheese. That's very popular now.'

'A *cheesecake*?' Mrs McCrae said, sounding hugely unimpressed. Helen opened her mouth, thought better of it and said nothing, to Maisie's surprise and relief.

'No, a stack of whole cheeses, like the tiers of a wedding cake, only made of cheese. They can look wonderful decorated with grapes and things, and people have them as the centrepiece of the buffet, or just as a huge cheeseboard to follow the meal. The bride and groom cut them in the normal way. You could source local cheeses—there are some wonderful ones apart from the Mull and

Orkney cheddars, and you could add others. Just a thought.'

'I really like that idea,' Alec said slowly, a smile dawning on his face, and Maisie let out a slow, quiet sigh of relief.

'So do I—and it's easily dealt with,' Rob said. 'Brilliant, Maisie. Thanks for that.'

'I sha' still make a wee fruit for 'e, it'll be expected,' Mrs McCrae muttered, stirring the pot as if she was beating the demons out of it, and then she smacked the spoon down and Maisie stifled a smile. 'Right, then, who's for Scotch broth? Or do you no' like that today, either?'

They tackled the rest of the things after lunch, until Jenni and Alec had to see the minister, and then Helen went to lie down for a while and Maisie and Rob were left alone together in the drawing room.

'So what else is there?'

She shrugged. 'I don't really know. I imagine table linen will be included in the table hire. Or do the caterers supply it with the crockery and glassware and so on?'

'Probably—to both. I'll get onto the hotel in the village and check they can do the catering, ring the marquee people for a quote and book the piper in the morning, and I need to track down a ceilidh band for the dance. There's one in the village and they're pretty good, but I don't know how Alec feels about them. We'd better ask.' He slumped against the chair back and shook his head slowly. 'There can't surely be much more, can there?'

'The order of service? Choosing a menu, then printing or ordering the menu cards, place names, table plan—that can only be done when you've got the replies—'

'Maisie, do you have to go back? I mean, I know you do, but couldn't you just go for the weddings and do the rest from here? I take it it's all digital?'

'Oh, of course, but I still have to talk them through with the couples afterwards and sort out their albums.'

'Can't you do that while you're down there doing other weddings, and then order them—you surely don't print them, do you?'

She shook her head. 'No. I edit them on my laptop, save them when the couple are happy and get the disk processed by a specialist firm. It's one of the joys of digital photography. And that's another point—we'll need a photographer. I wanted to talk to you about that.'

He lifted a brow. 'That's your department. Got any ideas?'

'Yes—and most of them involve me taking the shots!'

'No,' he said firmly, his eyebrows scrunching down in a frown. 'It's your daughter's wedding. You can't take the photos.'

'No, I know I can't, but I know a man who can,' she said with a slow smile, and Rob smiled back, the frown clearing.

'I was hoping you would. What about Jenni? What will she think of this other person?'

'She's happy. I've asked her. Now I just have to ask him, see if he's available. He might not be, in which case we'll have to think again, but I'll check with him tomorrow.'

She jotted it on her to-do list, then looked up at Rob. 'Anything else?'

'Not that I can think of. So is that the lot?'

'I believe so, for now.'

'Thank God,' he said, rolling his eyes. 'In which case, as it's a lovely day, why don't we go for a little stroll?'

She studied him warily. She knew him and his little strolls of old. 'Sure. Anywhere in particular?'

He shrugged. 'Wherever you like. I don't mind.'

'There was a glen you took me to, the first time I came up here with you. It was beautiful—so peaceful. I'd love to see it again, maybe take some photos, but I have no idea where it was and I don't suppose you remember.'

'I remember,' he said, his voice suddenly

slightly gruff. He cleared his throat and stood up, easing out the kinks in his shoulders with a hearty stretch that made her heart beat just a little faster. 'You'd better change into something warm— jeans and a jumper. I'll see if I can find you some boots. Will Jenni's fit you?'

'Oh—yes. We tend to share them.'

'I might have known you wouldn't have a pair of your own,' he teased, his voice soft now, and she huffed a little.

'I'll have you know I walk a lot!'

'On pavements. That doesn't count.'

'It most certainly does! I walk miles.'

But he just grinned, and said, 'Tell me that when you're at the top of the ridge,' and opening the door, he ushered her out, that smile still playing around his eyes and making her heart do funny things.

Things it should have got over years ago.

'Ten minutes,' he said. 'I'll meet you in the kitchen.'

And he disappeared off down the back stairs, leaving her to sort herself out.

It really was the most glorious day.

Rob had a small rucksack—'because I know you're going to want to take your fleece off'—and before they left, he smothered her in insect repellent.

She felt like a child, standing with her face upturned while he squirted Deet on his hands and rubbed them together, then wiped them over her cheeks, her brow, her temples, under her chin and down her throat, over the pulse that she knew was hammering under his fingertips.

But he couldn't have noticed, because there wasn't so much as a flicker of reaction, and when he'd done that he gave his hands another squirt and threaded them through her hair, gently massaging the spray into her scalp before stepping back and doing the same to himself before dropping the bottle into the rucksack.

'Right, let's go.'

He turned away, the dogs at his heels, and she followed him, her eyes fixed on his back, trying not to notice the flex of taut muscles as he strode up the steep slope behind the castle, heading for the path that they'd taken before.

She didn't think about his muscles for long, though, because her own took over in protest. After a short while she started breathing harder, then her thighs started to ache, and she concentrated on putting one foot in front of the other until they reached the top of the rise, by which time her thighs were screaming and Jenni's boots were beginning to rub.

She was hot, too, but there was no way she was

giving Rob her fleece to carry, so she tied it round her waist and slogged on without a word.

The way levelled out then, to her relief, running along the back of a ridge and heading out into the hills above the village. They were walking in woodland, scrubby trees and rhododendrons mostly, interspersed with conifers and gnarled, twisted birches with nothing but the odd scuttle in the undergrowth to disturb the peace. The path was broader here, and he held back until she fell into step beside him.

'OK?'

'I'm fine,' she lied, wishing she'd put thicker socks on. 'You?'

He eyed her fleece and gave her an enigmatic smile. 'I'm fine,' he echoed. They walked on in silence for a while, but unlike some of the silences they'd shared recently, this one was companionable.

'We used to do this a lot,' she said, after a while. 'Before Jenni.'

He gave a small grunt of acknowledgement, and draped his arm around her shoulders, giving her a brief hug. 'We did. Seems a long time ago. Lot of water under a lot of bridges.'

'Tell me about it,' she muttered, and she was just wondering if it would be a totally stupid idea to slide her arm round his waist when he dropped his and moved away, leaving her feeling ridiculously bereft.

But he was only heading up a narrow path, turning from time to time to help her up a tricky bit, and every time he did that, every time he wrapped his warm, hard hand around hers to steady her, she felt a jolt right down to her toes. Crazy. She had to keep this in perspective, remember that he was only doing this so they could be friends, looking to the future, to the time when they would be grandparents, though how they were meant to be grandparents when they'd hardly even managed to be parents was a mystery to her.

With any luck Jenni and Alec wouldn't be in any hurry to start a family, though, and maybe by the time they did she would have got her feelings for Rob under control.

Huh. Fat chance, she thought, and tripped over a root she'd failed to see. His hand flew out and steadied her, solid and reliable, there for her in the way he should have been all those years ago, and as she trudged after him she tried to work out when it had all gone wrong. Before Jenni, maybe? When he'd gone away to the navy and left her behind?

No. They'd been blissfully happy whenever he'd been at home, which had been quite frequently at first. It was only once he'd gone to sea that the gaps had been longer. Too long.

She gave a little shiver, suddenly oppressed by the trees, but then it opened out, the woodland giving way to glorious open country, glens and mountains stretching away in front of them, gilded by the spring sunshine, and they paused to take in the view while she got her breath back.

And it was spectacular. The colours were amazing in the sun. Greens and golds and purples and a rich, peaty brown—it was beautiful, as lovely as she'd remembered it, and she felt her heart lift. 'It's just stunning,' she said in awe, reaching for her camera, and he smiled.

'It is, isn't it? I never get tired of it.'

'Even in the rain?' she teased, turning to fire off some shots of him, but he just shook his head, his smile wry as she kept on shooting.

'Never. We need the rain. The whole ecosystem of the peat bogs and granite escarpments depends on it.'

'Including the midges,' she said, slapping her neck ruefully, and he pulled the bottle of insect repellent out again and reapplied it, his fingers firm and deft, setting her heart off again and sending shivers of aching need racing all over her body.

'You used to do this before,' she murmured, and his eyes darkened, locking with hers, the expression in them guarded. For what seemed like an age, they stood there, eyes locked, his pupils dark with some nameless emotion that made her want to cry.

'That was a long time ago, Maisie,' he said gruffly, and recapped the bottle as he stepped away from her, giving her room to breathe. He threw the bottle back in the rucksack, turned on his heel and set off again along the ridge, following the path to the head of the glen while she trailed behind him and cursed her stupid overactive hormones.

Except, of course, it was nothing to do with hormones, and everything to do with the fact that she still loved him, and always had.

CHAPTER SIX

HE could hear her breathing hard behind him, but never once did she make a murmur, and after another short climb he stopped and turned towards her.

She couldn't have been looking, her eyes trained on the path, and she cannoned into him, her soft, warm body colliding with his chest with a breathy 'Oomph', and his hands came up to catch her.

She felt so good. Too good, and holding her was making him ache for her all over again. He still hadn't got over holding her that morning, when he'd taken her into his arms and hugged her, and if he didn't let go of her soon, he wasn't going to be able to. He steadied her, then let her go, stepping back and dragging in some of the fresh, moist air before he did something stupid like kiss her.

'Still think you're fit?' he teased to get a rise out of her and lighten the atmosphere, but she just laughed grimly and tipped back her head and met his eyes in challenge, and heat slammed through him again.

'I'm fine,' she said determinedly, but he knew she wasn't. There'd been a hitch in her stride, just the merest suggestion of a limp, and he thought the boots might be rubbing.

'Good,' he said evenly, and shucking off the rucksack he sat down on a dry rock and pulled it open. 'I thought we could sit here and take in the view for a few minutes before we head back. I can't afford to be out too long, I've got things to do. Guests to see to.'

Guilt brushed her eyes, and he felt an echo of it clutch his gut. He was lying—partly to save her from herself, because he knew she would go on until she was on her knees, and partly because every cell in his body was screamingly aware of their isolation.

They were utterly alone, with only the dogs and the wildlife for company, and it was too tempting. Too—dammit—too dangerous. And he wanted to apologise for lying, but then he'd have to explain why, and he wasn't going there to save his life.

'I'm sorry. I didn't mean to take you away from your work,' she said, but he shook his head, the guilt eating him.

'Forget it. It was my idea to go for a walk. Here—present from Mrs McCrae.'

And he handed her a chunk of gingerbread, then poured two steaming mugs of tea while the dogs lined up and stared hopefully at them both, just in case. Just like him with Maisie.

'Not a chance,' he told them with irony as she reached for the tea, their fingers brushing and sending a current surging through him.

He pulled his hand back, shocked at the strength of his reaction. How could he still want her? After all this time, how could he still need her so badly? Because he did need her, and for two pins he'd have her back.

The realisation held him immobile for a second, but she didn't notice, she was staring out over the glen, her eyes soft-focused.

'It really is so beautiful here,' she said, her voice slightly awestruck, as if she'd only just remembered it. And maybe she had, he thought. Maybe, for the first time since she'd gone away, she was starting to remember the good times. And they had had good times—lots of them. He wondered if she was thinking about them. She wasn't even taking photographs, just soaking it all up, her expression rapt and somehow wistful as she turned to him.

'No wonder you love it so much.'

He nodded. He couldn't speak, because it wasn't the countryside he was looking at, it was Maisie, and he loved her so much it hurt.

Still, after everything, he loved her.

'We had some good times, didn't we, Rob?' she asked, her voice soft as she echoed his thoughts, and he nodded again.

'Yes, Maisie. We had some good times. Very good times.'

She sighed quietly. 'I loved you, Rob,' she murmured. 'I loved you so much, and I really thought you loved me. What went wrong?'

'I don't know.' It was the honest truth, perhaps the first time he'd faced it. Sitting here with her now, he realised he actually didn't know what had gone wrong. He'd always thought she'd walked away from a good marriage, but now he wasn't so sure. She'd walked away from a situation more intolerable than he'd realised, but there had been more wrong with it than that, and maybe they'd both assumed that love alone would have been enough to make it work.

And of course it wasn't enough. It needed work, effort, application on both sides. And it would have helped a whole lot if they hadn't both been kids.

She turned back, and then her eyes narrowed. 'Is that an eagle?' she asked, her voice soft, and he leant closer and peered along her arm, feeling her thrill as they watched the bird riding the thermals.

'Yes. The male, I believe.'

'Oh, why didn't I bring my long zoom with

me?' she wailed under her breath. 'I wish I had some binoculars—'

He was already reaching in the rucksack for them, and he pulled them out with a rueful grin. 'You wanted binoculars?'

She turned to look at him and started to laugh. 'What else have you got in there, Mary Poppins?' she asked him, and he gave a rusty chuckle and passed her the glasses.

'Oh, now, let me see, there's a standard lamp, and—'

'Idiot. Oh, I can't see it any more.'

'No. They're elusive and they blend incredibly well with the landscape. They're nesting over in the next glen, but it's hard to get to—which, of course, makes it a perfect choice as a nesting site, so you were very lucky to spot him, but it tends to frustrate the guests. There are lots of buzzards, though, and that tends to get them pretty excited when they mistake them for the eagles.' He grinned. 'We call them tourist eagles.'

She laughed softly. 'That's mean.'

'No, it's not. We don't lie to them, but if they come back all excited and tell us they've seen eagles and we know they'd be really disappointed if we told them the truth, we let them believe it, even though the buzzards are incredible in their own right. Beautiful birds, but the punters want eagles. It makes them happy, and we like happy customers.'

'Does that include me? Because if it wasn't an eagle, I'd rather you didn't lie to me. I think buzzards are just as lovely. They're one of the things I remember.'

His heart squeezed in his chest, and he managed a smile. 'I'm not lying to you, Maisie,' he assured her softly. 'It was definitely an eagle. I'm just not sure if it was the male or the female. The buzzards have different markings.'

'How can you see from that range?' she asked, and he chuckled quietly.

'One of the advantages of long sight. It makes up for the frustration of holding things at arm's length to read the small print.'

She smiled at that and turned back, scouring the glen for another glimpse of the magnificent bird, but it was gone, so she turned her attention to the gingerbread and he had to drag his eyes off her. Again.

'Jenni tells me you've been renting out the cottages to holidaymakers for a while now,' she said softly after a few minutes. 'How's it going?'

'Very well,' he said, nodding slowly. 'We do low-impact holidays—boat trips, guided walks, a little fishing, some deer stalking, but only with cameras, and the fishing's all catch and release. And to be fair the trout are pretty wily, so they don't get caught often. The visitors come for the walking and the wildlife, mostly, but they keep us out of mischief, and it pays the running costs of the estate. It can get a bit manic, though, in the summer, with them all wanting a piece of you at the same time.'

'How many cottages are there?'

'On the estate? Twelve, but Alec's parents have one, and the ghillie has one, and of course Jenni and Alec will have the gatehouse, so that leaves nine for letting, but two of those only sleep two.'

'And the rest?'

'The biggest takes eight. Our total capacity's forty, so in the summer Saturdays can be a bit crazy, but we have a brilliant team from the village who come and clean and turn them round. And once Jenni's up here she's going to be joining the team full time. We're going to use one of the rooms in the gatehouse as a reception and welcome centre for the guests as they arrive, a first point of contact, and that'll be her focus. She's going to be our front-of-house girl.'

'Yes, she mentioned that. She'll be good at it, I can see her doing that. She's got your easy charm with people, always has had. Maybe it's a shame she didn't study hospitality and tourism. It might have been more relevant than history.'

'No. She's enjoyed history, and it's equally appropriate. She's been working her way through the books in the library here, cataloguing them, and she's found all sorts of interesting old tomes. You ought to get her to show you if you get a moment before the wedding.'

The word seemed to bring her back down to earth with a bump. She chewed her lip, so that he wanted to reach out his thumb and soothe it, then kiss it better.

'This wedding,' she said, her brow puckering in a little frown.

He made himself concentrate. 'What about it?'

'It's a really busy time for you, isn't it?'

'Pretty busy. Still, it won't be a problem. The grounds are always kept tidy for the guests, and the house has been decorated from end to end in the last two years, so there isn't much to do in that way. And trust me, we'll have a fleet of staff to do all the to-ing and fro-ing. It'll be pretty painless, I think.'

Maisie wasn't so sure. She wondered if he'd missed the point, but she'd been to more weddings than he had and she had a better idea of what was in store. Let him think the worst was over for now. There was plenty of time to disillusion him.

'Still, I didn't realise the planning would be such a killer,' he went on, his smile wry.

'I bet you thought it would all be over in a day.'

'That long? Try five minutes.'

Maisie laughed until her sides ached, then sighed softly, wishing they'd had more moments like this, moments of humour. Maybe then they could have made it work, been there for each other when things had gone wrong. 'Well, as I said before, we'll only have to do this once.' She studied him thoughtfully, but his eyes were veiled so she couldn't see their expression. 'Does that worry you? I know what you said this morning, that one is more than enough, but I've often wondered if you mind that your only child is a girl?'

He shook his head slowly. 'No. No, I don't mind. I love her to bits, and I wouldn't change her for anything. And I don't think she's suffered from being an only child. I was an only child, and it has advantages in some ways, but—well, whatever. I would have liked more, but you don't always get what you want and I'm not complaining.'

'You could have married again—had a son to hand the estate on to. I should've thought you'd want that.'

He shot her an enigmatic look. 'No, Maisie. I haven't, I didn't, and I'm not about to now. And I don't need a son. I've got Alec, and I've got a lot of time for him. He's done well for himself, worked hard, and he knows the farm inside out. And he's taken it very seriously—he's got two degrees now, in agricultural science and agro-management, he's very into expanding our potential. He's a real asset. I'm proud of him—and, no, I didn't have a son of my own, but Alec is the next best thing, and I'm more than happy that he's marrying our little girl.'

He eyed her thoughtfully. 'Anyway, you can talk. What about you? I would have thought you'd marry again, have more children. You always said you wanted lots of babies, but maybe having Jenni put you off.'

'No. Not at all,' she said quietly, thinking of the babies they might have had together—the only babies she'd ever wanted. There'd been men she'd met over the years, decent men, men who'd tried to persuade her to have a relationship. Men who might have married her. But they hadn't been Rob, and he was the only man she wanted. The only man she'd ever wanted.

'If I'd wanted more children, I could easily have had more,' she told him matter-of-factly. 'Children are easy to get, Rob. It's bringing them up and dealing with the emotional fallout that's the hard bit. But if you're asking if I regret that our relationship didn't work, that she didn't have two parents in the same place and siblings and a more normal family life, then the answer's yes. But it didn't happen, and no amount of regret's going to change that.'

She turned her head to meet his eyes, and saw a flash of pain in their slate-blue depths.

'No,' he said, his voice quietly sincere, filled with a sorrow she knew was as deep as hers. He reached out and cupped her face in his warm, slightly roughened palm, his thumb stroking lightly over her cheek as he held her eyes.

'I never should have let you go,' he said gruffly. 'I should have followed you, made you talk to me. I should have found a way for us to be together somehow. Why the hell didn't I, Maisie? Why the hell didn't I come after you?'

She swallowed hard, then closed her eyes. 'I don't know, Rob. I have no idea at all.'

She emptied her cup out onto the grass, handed it back to him and stood up, wincing at her aching muscles and wondering how she'd thought she was fit. Wondering about anything except why he hadn't followed her, because that hurt too much to think about.

'Come on, Mackenzie,' she said, turning her back on him and heading down the track towards the castle. 'I thought you had things to do?'

They went to church the next morning, listened to the banns being read from their position in the Laird's loft up above the congregation, and then they were subjected to a hail of congratulations and good wishes from the people of the village. As a consequence it took an age to get away, and by the time they got back to the castle it was time for lunch.

Mercifully, because it meant there was less time to talk, and the less time they had, the better. The tension was simmering between them, and every time she caught Rob's eye, it was as if he was staring right down inside her, looking for an answer.

Well, he wouldn't find it in her, she was sure. She didn't know the answer. She wasn't even sure she knew the question. But despite the tension, they got done everything that could be done over the weekend, and all that remained was a few calls to make the following day. So Rob booked her return sleeper on the Sunday evening, with her standing beside him at his desk in the study overlooking the sea, and she watched the last dying rays of the evening sun stretch across the endless sky, and wondered why she was going back so soon.

It didn't seem so imperative any more, and she found she had a curious reluctance to leave. Not that it was easy, with the tension between them pulling them every which way, and maybe it would be better to be apart just now, let the new, tentative friendship between them settle into their lives without pushing it. Or jeopardising it with some hasty and ill-considered action.

Like resting her hand on his shoulder, stooping

down and pressing a kiss to his thick, dark hair with its little threads of silver that somehow made him even more attractive. Like tilting his face back and pressing her lips to his, turning to sit on his lap and sliding her arms around his neck…

'Right, that's that done,' he said, pushing back his chair and turning to look up at her, and she met his eyes and smiled somehow.

'Thank you.'

'You don't have to go,' he said, as if he was reading her mind. 'I can change it to a later date.'

She shook her head before she could let him talk her out of it. 'No, Rob, I need to get back. I've got things to do. We both have.'

By the time she set off the following evening, the rest of the arrangements were falling neatly into place. The hotel was booked for the catering, they were going to the hotel that night for a food tasting, something Maisie was sure they could do without her, and the piper and ceilidh band were booked. And Jeff was free to take the photographs, to her immense relief, because he was the only person she trusted to take the sort of shots she would have taken herself. She had lots of pictures of the castle and grounds, the ruin—and Rob, of course, taken on their walk. She'd put them into a separate file.

He took her to the station, put her on the train

and then hesitated, standing in the tiny little cabin so that she felt all the air had been sucked out of it.

His face was troubled, his eyes guarded, and for a moment they stood there and looked at each other in silence.

Then he reached for her and pulled her gently into his arms, enfolding her against his chest so she could feel the steady, even beating of his heart. 'Thank you for coming,' he murmured. 'And I'm sorry about all the things that have happened. I didn't realise it had been so hard for you here, and I'm really grateful for your help. I'm so glad you came.'

'I had no choice, Rob. I did it for Jenni,' she reminded him gently, and he gave a quiet sigh and let her go, holding her shoulders, staring down into her eyes with an expression she couldn't quite understand.

'Don't leave it too long before you're back,' he said, and ducking his head he brushed his lips lightly over hers, turned on his heel and strode away.

She closed the door and sat down abruptly on the bunk. Her lips tingled, and she lifted her hand and touched her fingertips to the place where his lips had been so fleetingly.

Not fleetingly enough. Her lips were still tingling when the train pulled out of the station over half an hour later, at the start of the long journey away from him.

And not, it seemed, before time.

Life got back to normal, slowly, but somehow it didn't feel quite the same.

There were the flowers, for a start.

They arrived the day she got back, a beautifully presented hand-tied posy of spring flowers, simple and delicate but absolutely perfect. There was a card, written in a woman's hand, of course, not his dark, slashing script that was all but illegible. It said, quite simply, 'Rob. X'

A kiss. Just the one, like the kiss he'd feathered across her lips on the train just last night. She pressed her lips together, sniffed the flowers— they smelled gorgeous, a taste of spring—and she set them in the middle of the dining table that served as her desk, so she could look at them as she worked.

Look at them and think of him.

She had a phone call later in the week, and the first thing she did was thank him for them.

'My pleasure,' he murmured, and she felt the words cruise over her nerve endings like a dancing flame.

'So, how are things?' she asked, picturing him

in his study, feet up on the old desk, the sea view stretched out in front of him.

'Fine. Jenni's back at uni, the dress is hanging up in her bedroom here, wrapped in a cloth cover as instructed, we've got the veil and everyone's happy,' Rob reported.

'How was the food tasting?'

'Good. We're still deciding, but the standard is excellent. We were very pleased. And otherwise I think all the arrangements are under way. How about you?'

'Oh, I'm busy. I'm up to my eyes. You were lucky to catch me, I'm just going out to meet a bride to talk wedding photos.'

'Well, I won't hold you up. Take care.'

'You, too.'

She put the phone down, thinking that even a fortnight ago such a phone call would have been unheralded. Brief though it had been, it was another plank on the bridge they were building, and as she raced off for her meeting, his voice was carried with her in her head.

She was ridiculously busy for the next few weeks, both with her photography and with features for the paper. They found out at the office that her daughter was getting married, and immediately sent her to cover a society wedding.

Then there was a spread about the cost of

getting married, with budget and lavish options. It was an eye-opener, even for her with all the weddings she'd been involved in.

So was her bank statement. She hadn't looked at the prices when she'd paid for Jenni's dress and her outfit, but she could see the amount on the statement now, and she pulled the receipt out of her handbag and studied it, and winced.

Never mind. Jenni would look stunning in the dress, and she'd been thrilled with her mother's outfit.

Maisie herself still wasn't sure about it. It hung in the wardrobe, waiting for her to find time to accessorise it—or alternatively replace it with something less, well, less likely to 'blow Dad's socks off', as Jenni had so subtly put it.

She didn't want to blow his socks off. Far too dangerous. And after that kiss on the train, however brief and fleeting, she wondered just how easy it might be. She'd felt a simmering energy in him in the last few days of her visit, a raw, untamed side that she'd never seen before, and it thrilled her and terrified her all at once.

But going there would be potentially more foolish now than it had been twenty-one years ago, so she had no intention of poking the sleeping tiger.

Except maybe he wasn't sleeping, just lying with one eye slightly open, waiting for an unwary move. And, meanwhile, the dress hung in her wardrobe, taunting her. So she ignored it, put the wedding out of her mind and concentrated on her work. Until Rob phoned again.

'Maisie.'

Just the one word, but all her senses were on red alert, her body humming.

'Hi. Problems?'

'No, not exactly. Look, I'm in London, I had one or two things to do, but I'm finished now—can I come and see you? I've got the invitations, and you said you'd write them, so I thought I could drop them off with the guest list—and there are one or two other details. I thought maybe we could discuss them over dinner, if you aren't busy?'

'I thought the details were sorted? Does it really need dinner?' she asked, panicking a little because dinner…well, it sounded a little bit like a date, and she wasn't at all sure she was ready for a date with Robert Mackenzie.

'No, not really, I suppose. I could just drop the invitations off, have a quick run-through of my thoughts and then set off again, but I have to eat at some point, and…' She almost heard the shrug, and then he carried on, 'Anyway, I thought we were supposed to be making friends.'

They were. She thought of their grandchildren,

years down the line, and sighed inwardly. She'd just have to keep a lid on her feelings, however hard it was. 'Of course. Sorry. Yes, that sounds OK. I'm not busy tonight.'

'Great. Do you want me to make a reservation somewhere, or will you do it?'

'I'll do it,' she said quickly. She couldn't trust him not to find somewhere—romantic. Intimate. She'd book a table in a noisy, bustling place—she didn't want him getting any wrong ideas, and romantic and intimate were definitely wrong.

'Thanks. That would make sense. And then I can set off tomorrow morning early for the drive home—if you don't mind putting me up, that is.'

He wanted to *stay*? Her heart flipped and started to race, and a million excuses ran through her head, but they were exactly that, excuses, and she had agreed to do the invitations. And dinner. And be friends. But *stay*? After that kiss?

'Of course you can stay,' she said at last. 'You can have Jenni's room. It's your house, after all.'

'Hardly. It's not been my house for the last twenty years.'

'That's a technicality,' she said, and there was a second's silence.

'Maisie, it's your *home*,' he said, sounding stunned.

'Well, whatever,' she said quietly, her emotions

tumbling. It was her home—of course it was her home, but at the same time, Rob haunted it, the memory of him soaked into the very fabric, so that she'd never felt she could do certain things in it. Things like take a lover, and bring him back to her bedroom, the room where she'd made love with Rob, so that she could try and erase him from her memory. Not that there had ever been anyone.

'Look, I'm busy, I don't need to get into this now, I'm due out. What time are you coming?'

'I thought I'd leave now. I want to get out of London before the traffic builds up. I should be with you by one at the latest. Is that OK?'

'I should be back. I've got to go and deliver an album to someone. Have you got your key still?'

'Not with me. Don't worry, if you aren't there I can amuse myself. Just call me when you're done. I'll see you later.'

'OK. I'll see you,' she said, wondering how long she'd be.

She looked at her watch. Nine thirty-nine—so nearly ten. She was due with Annette at ten-thirty, but she phoned her to find out if she could come earlier, and was greeted with delight.

'Of course! I'm longing to see the albums, I can't believe you've got them printed so quickly. Do come now. I'll put the kettle on.'

She was there just after ten, and Annette greeted

her at the door in a flowing caftan with a bandana round her head.

'Hi, come in, it's lovely to see you,' she said, and kissed Maisie on the cheek. 'Coffee?'

'That would be lovely. How are you?'

'Oh, you know,' she said, wrinkling her nose. 'I'm halfway through my first chemo, and my hair's started to come out in clumps already so I've had it shaved, but I'm too old to look interesting and elegant, so I've wrapped it up and gone ethnic instead! But my scan was clear, no more hot spots, so things are looking good. Fingers crossed. Biscuit?'

'Oh, I shouldn't but I don't care. Yes, please!'

They chuckled as Annette raided a cupboard and produced some utterly wicked chocolate biscuits, poured boiling water into the cafetière and headed through to the sitting room. 'Right, let's see these albums. I can't wait.'

They were in the style of a coffee-table book, with some pages containing just one image, and others containing several scattered casually over the page. And there were some gorgeous ones of Annette with her daughter.

'Oh, Maisie, it's wonderful! Oh, thank you so much,' Annette said, sniffing and mopping her eyes. 'Oh, how silly of me. I'm sorry, I feel really overwhelmed by them, you've really captured the day, they're beautiful, and I just love having them in a real book. Oh, thank you so much. You've been so kind and understanding.'

'Don't be silly. It's been a pleasure working with you all and getting to know you, and I'm thrilled with them. In fact, I've stolen some of the ideas for my daughter Jenni's wedding.'

'She's getting married? Oh, how exciting! When? You haven't mentioned it.'

'June. I found out the day before Lucy's wedding—she just phoned up and announced they were getting married in eleven weeks! So I've been stealing ideas right, left and centre!'

'Of course you have—and it's perfectly possible to do in that time. We did it in less, and I don't think it could have been better for another year of preparation. Oh, I'm so thrilled for you, I do hope you have a fabulous day. So where's the wedding?'

She pulled a face. 'In Scotland—just north-west of Fort William. I'd rather it was here, of course, but that's just unrealistic, and Ardnashiel's a fabulous location.'

Annette's eyes narrowed thoughtfully and she tipped her head on one side. 'Not the castle?'

'Yes—her father owns it,' she admitted.

Her eyes widened, and she smiled delightedly. 'Robert Mackenzie's her father?'

Maisie was startled. 'Yes—do you know him?' she asked, surprised.

'I lectured him years ago. Must be—twenty-something? So did you meet him here?'

Maisie pulled a face. 'Yes. Just after he graduated. I went to look at his house, and we—well, we ended up getting married a little hastily. Jenni was the result. It—er—it didn't work out, though.'

Annette made a soft sound of commiseration and squeezed her hand. 'Oh, I'm sorry. I've been so lucky in that way. Did you marry again?'

'No. No, once was enough.'

'So he was the only one for you?'

Her eyes filled and she looked away quickly. 'Well, you know him. He's that kind of person, really. Hard to follow.'

'Yes, I can imagine. He was a brilliant student—I always wondered what happened to him. So has he inherited the estate now?'

'Yes.'

'Which must make him the Laird, of course.'

Maisie nodded. 'Yes. And, of course, that rather dictates the wedding. It's not very convenient for me, with all the long-distance planning, but it's better for everybody else, and even if we could find a better setting, it wouldn't be right for Jenni to get married in any other place.'

'No—and I imagine it's beautiful. He talked

about it once or twice—it sounded as if he really loved it, as if it filled his soul.'

She nodded again, amazed that Annette remembered him so well. 'I think it does, and it is beautiful, especially the countryside around there. I felt that more this time than I have before—I've always found it a bit daunting in the past. It's gorgeous in the summer, but it can be a bit bleak in the winter, and the castle was a bit austere then. He's made lots of changes, though, and it's much more welcoming.'

'There was a dungeon, wasn't there?'

'Oh, yes. I'd forgotten that. It's got a slit in the wall, high up, so the smells from the kitchen could drift down and torment the prisoners. I used to lie awake and wonder how many of the kitchen staff threw food to them, and what it was like down there.'

'Horrible, I expect. The warring Highland clans could be pretty uncompromising. Not that Robert was ever like that.'

'Oh, he can be,' she said softly, wondering if that was why he hadn't followed her. 'Compromise isn't exactly his middle name—but he's learning! The wedding's forcing him to, and he's a good father. He's taking all the wedding stuff very well.'

Annette chuckled. 'It can be a bit full on, can't it?' Her smile faded. 'I'd love to see him again. I was always very fond of him.'

'I'm amazed you remember him.'

'Oh, Robert was unforgettable. As you said yourself.'

So true. Maisie took a slow breath and tried not to dwell on that. 'He's down here at the moment, actually. He had some things to do in London, and he's on the way here now to drop some things off and sort out a few details. Would you like me to ask him to pop in while he's in Cambridge?'

Her eyes lit up, but then she shook her head. 'Oh, he won't remember me.'

'I'm sure he will. I'll ask him—if you like.'

'Would you? I would love to see him, but only if he's got time.'

'I'll ask him.' She could see Annette was flagging, so she gathered her things and stood up. 'I'll leave you in peace now. I ought to be getting back. I'll get him to ring and arrange a time to visit you, if you like?'

'Would you? Thank you so much—and thank you again for the photographs. I know I've said it before, but it was a real pleasure to have you there, and you couldn't possibly have done a better job. We were all thrilled.'

'Oh, Annette, bless you. It was a real privilege to share it with you.' She stooped to kiss her cheek, and then let herself out and drove home.

That word again.

Odd, how it could be home and yet still feel like his house, as if the bricks and mortar held the memory of his presence. No wonder she'd never moved on.

His car was outside when she pulled up, and he was sitting there with the roof down, his head tipped back and his eyes shut, listening to the radio.

'You made good time,' she said, pausing by the car, and he opened one eye and sat up.

'Yeah, the road was good. Am I in your space?'

She laughed. 'There's no such thing as my space. I park wherever I can. Here, take my permit and put it in your windscreen or you'll get a ticket. I'll be back in a minute.'

That was one of the disadvantages of being in a university town as steeped in history as Cambridge was. She was right in the thick of the colleges, close to the river and handy for the town. Any spaces going were either metered or occupied by residents, but her neighbours allowed her to park in their drive, and she turned in there now and headed back to him.

The hood was up now, and he was propped against the car, his long legs crossed at the ankle, a soft leather case at his feet and a heavy-duty carrier bag in his hand.

'Invitations?'

'Amongst other things.' He picked up his case

and followed her up the little path to the front door, then into the little terraced house that she didn't feel was hers.

Crazy, he thought. Why hadn't she told him? He'd had no idea that she felt like that—no idea about so many things, he admitted. His mother, for instance, and the way she'd been to Maisie while he'd been at sea.

'Jenni sends her love,' he said as she closed the door behind them.

'How is she? I spoke to her the other day, she sounded a bit hassled.'

'She is. She's been working hard. The dress is lovely, by the way. It looks shockingly expensive.'

She laughed, a little rueful smile playing around her mouth. 'It was,' she admitted. 'But I wanted to do it for her, and it's absolutely gorgeous on.'

'I know. I saw it. I went with them. Mum was very pleased to be included, by the way, and she was delighted with the veil.'

'Which one did she go for?' Maisie asked, unpacking a bag and piling stuff into the fridge.

'Long—very simple. She said she wants some photos up in the ruined tower. She thought the long one, blowing in the wind, could make some spectacular photos.'

'She's right. I'll brief Jeff before the day.'

He laughed and propped himself against the worktop so he could see her face. 'I'm sure you will,' he said drily.

She arched a brow and walked away, putting the kettle on. 'Talking of photos, I've got a message for you from Annette Grainger.'

He did a mild double-take. 'Really? Dr Grainger? How do you know her?' he asked.

'She's the mother of the bride I told you about—the one starting chemo.'

He felt a wave of denial. 'Oh, no. Not her.'

'It's OK, it's not looking too bad. Her scan's come back clear, and she's sounding hopeful. She said she'd love to see you again. I told her I'd get you to ring her.'

'Sure. I'd love to see her. Should I call her now?'

'No, better leave it for a while. She was looking tired—that's where I was just now. She's probably resting. Call her later, before we go out.'

She pulled two mugs out and set them on the worktop. 'I didn't know what you wanted for lunch, so I grabbed a few things—pre-prepared salads, that sort of thing. I thought I'd keep it simple if we're going out tonight.'

He nodded, then shrugged away from the side and rammed his hands in his pockets to keep them out of mischief. He didn't want to think about tonight. 'How do you fancy a picnic?'

'A picnic?'

'Mmm. I thought we could go punting.'

'Punting?' she said, as if he'd suggested eating underwater, and then she smiled slowly, her eyes soft. 'I haven't been punting for years. I went a few years ago, with Jenni and Alec, but I was so busy watching them together and trying to deal with their blindingly obvious devotion to each other that I didn't really take it in. Before then—well, that was really years ago.'

Twenty-something? He didn't want to go there, so he stuck to Jenni and Alec. 'So—how do you feel about them now? Are you more accepting of their relationship?' he asked, and she nodded.

'Oh, yes,' she said calmly. 'I've always been happy about their relationship, it was just getting married so young, but having seen them together in Scotland—well, you're right, they fit together as if they were made for each other. I still think they're very young but, as you say, they know each other inside out, and better this way than the way we did it.'

Her words hung in the air, the tension suddenly ratcheting up a notch, and he let out a short sigh and nodded.

'Yes. I agree. So—picnic on a punt?'

She pulled herself together. 'Yes—sure. Let's see what I've got.'

She hauled everything out of the fridge again, and they made ham salad rolls with a dollop of coleslaw, and packed them up with some cold barbecued chicken legs and juicy cherry tomatoes and a packet of hand-cooked crisps. Then she added a pack of fresh cream chocolate éclairs, and he started to chuckle.

'Well, I suppose the tomatoes are healthy,' he teased, and she blushed and pulled out a bottle of mineral water.

'I wasn't really thinking. I just grabbed stuff quickly. If you're going to complain…'

'I'm not complaining!' he said, throwing his hands up and trying not to laugh. 'Really, I'm not complaining. I'm starving, I missed breakfast because I was working late and overslept. It looks great.'

'Well, we'd better go, then,' she said, zipping up the cool bag, and he took it from her and ushered her out of the door.

They walked the short distance to the river, arriving just as a punt was being returned. 'Two hours?' he asked her, and she nodded.

'One's not enough, not if we're going to take time to enjoy it,' she said, and then wondered if two hours alone on a boat with him would be such a good idea after all.

Except, of course, they were hardly alone. They

were surrounded by rank amateurs, and college students taking guided punts to earn a bit of extra money, and on a lovely early May Saturday, the river was heaving.

They set off, him balancing easily on the stern, her sitting in the bows facing him. She had the best view from there. She could watch the river go by, and as an added bonus she could watch Rob, his muscles moving smoothly under the soft jersey shirt he was wearing, his thighs braced as he pushed away from the wall to avoid a group of girls who were wildly out of control.

They looked like girls on a hen weekend, Maisie thought, looking at their silly printed T-shirts and the glasses of champagne, and she wondered what Jenni was doing for hers, if anything.

The punt jolted, and the girls giggled, the girl standing on the back wobbling wildly and letting out a little shriek.

'Steady,' Rob said, grabbing her arm as she flailed, and she straightened up and flashed him a smile that made Maisie want to scratch her eyes out.

'Sorry!' She giggled, and hit the wall again.

He shook his head and smiled at Maisie. 'Kids.'

Kids? There was nothing of the child in that young woman's look, she thought, and wondered if he'd even noticed. Possibly not. She was about Jenni's age, maybe a little older, and it was quite gratifying that he wasn't eyeing her up, because she was very pretty.

'Just because you're so darned good at it,' she said drily, and he grinned and ducked to go under another bridge.

'All that practice. It's great for impressing the girls.'

She knew that. As a girl she'd been very impressed by his skill with the punt. Very impressed with his skill with everything, come to that.

She looked away hastily, studying the backs of the colleges, seeing them as you only did from the river.

'Shall we tie up here?' he suggested when they reached an area of open grass, and they secured the punt to the rings on the side and climbed out, settling down on the grass with the cool bag.

He handed her a roll, and she ate it staring out across the river Cam, studying the glorious architecture of the ancient colleges and wishing things had been different, wishing that they'd settled here, that he'd never joined the navy, that they'd had more children and Ardnashiel had never been part of their lives.

She ripped open the crisps and dropped a handful in her lap, then picked up a chicken leg.

'Penny for them.'

'Not a chance,' she said, and sank her teeth into the chicken.

CHAPTER SEVEN

HE didn't know what to make of her.

No surprises there, he never did know what to make of her. Never had. But today—one minute she was sitting there watching him in the boat and laughing with him at the antics of some of the punters, the next she looked as if her best friend had kicked her puppy.

And she clearly didn't want to talk about it, so he ignored her, lay down on his back on the fresh spring grass and listened to the sound of laughter, the odd shriek or splash, hasty apologies as punts collided with dull thuds. He could hear children playing, people strolling past, a dog barking in the distance. And Maisie rustling in the bag.

'Want an éclair?'

He opened one eye and peered up at her. She was dangling one above his face, just out of reach, and so just for the hell of it he opened his mouth and waited.

And waited.

And then she lowered it, putting the end in his mouth so he could bite it off, the soft, squashy pastry giving way so the cream oozed out and smeared on his lips. He licked them, and her eyes widened slightly. And as he watched her, she took a bite herself, and the sensual imagery slammed through him.

'Hey, that's mine,' he said, sitting up abruptly to take the rest of it from her before she could blow his mind, but she just laughed and took another bite and handed him the box.

'Have your own,' she said through a mouthful of cream, and then licked her fingers.

She was trying to kill him.

He took one and ate it sitting up, one leg drawn up and his arm curled round his knee, avoiding looking at her and eating it systematically and—almost impossibly—without licking his lips. Or his fingers.

He wiped them instead on a tissue, and still didn't look at her. He wasn't playing that game any more. Too dangerous. He'd end up making a fool of himself over her, and he'd done that once before and had never got over it. He wasn't doing it again.

'So, where does Annette live now?' he asked, and the conversation moved to safer topics.

* * *

He went alone to see Annette. He took her flowers—green and white, on Maisie's advice—and rang the bell.

She opened the door almost instantly, as if she'd been waiting for him, and her face lit up.

'Rob! Oh, how lovely to see you. Oh, I would have known you anywhere. You've hardly changed at all—well, except your hair.'

He grinned at her. 'Well, you can talk,' he said gently, touching the colourful fabric wrapped around her head, and she laughed and reached her arms up and hugged him.

'Bad boy. And you've brought me flowers. How lovely, thank you. They're beautiful. Come on in and tell me all about yourself while I put them in water. I gather you and Maisie have a daughter? You are a dark horse. The last thing I heard you were off to the navy.'

'Yes. I did six years in the submarines.'

And in hindsight, although it had been a valuable and humbling experience and had taught him a great deal about himself, it had probably been the most foolish mistake of his life. Hindsight was a wonderful thing.

He talked to Annette about his business in London, still ticking over nicely in the background, about the castle and the estate, about

Jenni and the wedding—and then she asked about Maisie.

'What went wrong?' she said.

He nearly didn't answer, nearly told her to mind her own business, but she'd always had time for him, always listened to him, always been there for him.

'I don't know,' he said at last. 'It was after she had Jenni. I was away, I missed the birth, but things were never the same after that. She— I don't know, she didn't seem to want me, although maybe it started earlier than that. Our marriage didn't get the best of starts.'

'No, she implied it was a bit hasty.'

'Yes. We'd found out she was pregnant. Getting married seemed like a good idea at the time, but we didn't know each other nearly well enough then, of course.'

'And later, when you knew each other better?'

He looked away. 'I'm not sure we ever did. I was away a lot, she was unhappy, and she left, came back to Cambridge.'

'And you let her go.'

'I had nothing to offer her that she wanted.'

'Are you sure? Because that's not the impression I got,' Annette suggested softly, but he shook his head.

'She shut me out. She didn't want me.'

'But, like you, she's never married anyone else, never found another man to make her happy. And when I asked her why, she told me you were hard to follow. Doesn't that tell you something?'

He searched her eyes—kind, sage eyes that had seen so much—and he sighed.

'We're different, Annette. We want different things. She hates Ardnashiel.'

'I don't think she hates it, Rob. I think she was unhappy there, but she spoke quite fondly of it today. Said you'd done a lot to it, and it was much less austere.'

'Well, I've done a bit. It'll never be finished, places like that never are, but I love it. It's home, but Maisie never felt like that. It has bad associations for her. I know it was difficult for her being up there with a small baby while I was away, and I've discovered that my parents didn't make it easy for her. I didn't realise that before. But it's too late for us, Annette. She's built a life for herself here now.'

She leant forward and touched his arm, her fingers gentle. 'Maybe you should try again. Maybe she was waiting for you to ask her, and you didn't. Maybe that was what went wrong.'

Could she be right? Had Maisie simply been waiting for him to follow her, to ask her what had gone wrong so they could put it right?

Maybe. He'd begun to wonder—but that had been a long time ago, and now they had the wedding to get through. Not the time to start dragging skeletons out of cupboards.

Nevertheless, the thought played on his mind as he made his farewells and drove back to Maisie's house. He'd lost his parking place, of course, but it was after six and he found a slot around the corner and went back to find her in her dressing gown in the kitchen, making tea.

'I've just had a shower—I thought I'd do that while you were out so the water had time to heat up again for you. Tea?'

He dragged his eyes off the gaping V of her dressing gown. 'Please. Is there a dress code for this place tonight?'

'Not really. Smart casual? What you've got on would do. So, how did you get on with Annette? Did you recognise her?'

He smiled. 'Oh, yes, of course. She's hardly changed. She spoke very highly of you—and she showed me the wedding photos. They were—well, amazing, really. They took me by surprise. I had no idea you were so gifted.'

She gave him a level look. 'Have you ever checked my website? You probably didn't even know I had one.'

He felt a prickle of guilt, 'I did, but I haven't

looked at it.' Avoided it, more like, as he avoided anything to do with her on the grounds of damage limitation, but she didn't know that and she took it as disinterest, if the expression on her face was anything to go by.

'Ah, well, there you go. Perhaps you should have done,' she said tartly. 'Here, your tea.'

And plonking it down in front of him, she took hers and disappeared upstairs with it, closing her bedroom door firmly.

He made a mental note to check her website, and retreated to the sitting room—not the room at the front which he had used and which he saw now she was using as a study, but the room at the back, overlooking the pretty little courtyard garden. She'd made it quite lovely, he realised, a lush little oasis. It was filled with pots and tubs, and although it wasn't the sunniest, the late afternoon sun slanted in and filtered through the leaves of the nearby trees, dappling it with a soft, gentle light.

He'd always loved the garden, and they'd intended to put in doors from this room. They'd talked about it years ago, when they'd first met, and he wondered why she'd never done it. Money? Or because she still felt as if it was his house?

He frowned. That was so silly, but also so typical. She'd always been very sensitive to atmosphere. Maybe she'd never really liked the house?

In which case she should have sold it and moved on.

He sighed, took his empty mug through to the kitchen and then went upstairs. Her door was firmly shut, but she was probably getting ready. Good thing. That dressing gown was just a quick tug away from leaving her naked, and even the thought was enough to scramble what was left of his brains.

He went into Jenni's bedroom, opened his case and found his wash things, then went to have a shower.

A cold one.

She had no idea what to wear.

Jeans and a top? A long, casual skirt? A smart little dress? Or the khaki…?

Jeans, she decided. She was pretty sure the restaurant didn't have a dress code. Although if they did…

OK, not jeans. Trousers? Not a pretty little evening dress. Not something that would leave her legs on show.

She opened the wardrobe and there was the wedding outfit, hanging there in its exclusive little garment bag, tormenting her. *It'll blow Dad's socks off!* She grabbed her plain black trousers, shut the door hastily and leant back against it.

Right, so, trousers, and—a jumper? She had a pretty one, but it wasn't really dressy and it might be too warm. A blouse? She had a new one she'd never worn.

She put the trousers back in the wardrobe and pulled out the long linen shift, in a muddy khaki that went with her eyes. It skimmed the tops of her feet, covered the legs that definitely didn't need to be on display—he'd always had a thing about her legs—and she could wear a little cardi over the top. It was her favourite garment at the moment, the thing she fell back on when all else failed. She could dress it up or down, and it was clean. Always an advantage.

She pulled it over her head, zipped it up and dragged a brush through her hair, then looked at herself. A touch of make-up, perhaps—not much, she didn't tend to wear a great deal, but somehow none at all was unlikely and at the very least she always wore tinted moisturiser and mascara.

With a resigned shrug, she put on what she would have worn for a night out with the girls, and stood back, eyeing herself critically. Hmm. She wouldn't want him thinking she'd made too much effort. So just a touch of lipstick. And a spritz of cologne.

Necklace? No. Beads—chunky beads, burnt

orange ones to go with that little cardi she'd picked up the other day.

She eyed herself again, then nodded. Job done. She was reaching for the door knob when there was a tap on the door.

'Maisie? I'm ready when you are. Are we going in the car, or is it nearby?'

'It's near,' she said, opening the door. 'We can walk.'

'Good.' He ran his eye over her and smiled. 'You look lovely.'

So did he, but it would have choked her to say so.

'It's just an old dress,' she said dismissively, ridiculously pleased and refusing to show it because she was still mad with him for never having checked out her website, and she wasn't letting him off the hook that easily. Oh, no.

She took a step forward to leave her room and walked into the space he'd occupied a second earlier. A space filled with his fragrance. Oh, he smelt good. Citrus and spice and raw male. Thankfully they were walking and she wasn't going to be trapped inside a car with him!

But as she locked the front door behind them and set off for the restaurant at a brisk pace, he fell into step beside her, and with her first breath her hopes of escaping that subtle, sexy scent were blown instantly out of the water.

* * *

'So—the wedding,' Maisie said when their food had arrived and she was picking through the pasta with a fork. 'You wanted to talk to me about it?'

He put his fork down and picked up his wine, swirling it slowly in the glass. 'Yes. Nothing much, just a few details I don't want to trouble Jenni with. Timings, really, and I thought you've been to lots of weddings, presumably, so you know how they work.'

She nodded. 'OK. I can give you a rough time-table—is this for the caterers?'

'Yes, and the ceilidh band. Oh, and I wanted to talk to you about catering. We had the food tasting.'

'How was it?'

He wrinkled his nose. 'Not sure. Very good food, but I wasn't sure about the balance of the dishes. Jenni and Alec couldn't agree, and they gave me the casting vote, so I thought when you're next up there, perhaps we should go and check it out and you can tell me what you think.'

That sounded to Maisie like another dinner date, but she didn't argue, just nodded agreement and let it go. 'OK.'

'And we were wondering about canapés with the reception drinks. We've got two hours to fill. Do you think we need them?'

'It's up to you. I think they're nice, but they can be expensive.'

He dismissed that with a wave of his hand. 'We aren't talking about a cast of thousands, and in the great scheme of things it's just a drop in the ocean. So I'll email you a list of the options, and could you give me your thoughts?'

'Sure. Is that it?'

'Flowers.'

'Ah. Did Jenni and your mother sort themselves out in the end? She was so set on the monochrome thing, and I don't think she'd even considered having a colour in the flowers. I know she's settled on creams and lilacs now, but was it an amicable compromise in the end?'

He sighed and gave a weary smile. 'I think so. My mother wasn't being awkward, you know, she was genuinely upset.'

'I know that.' Maisie sighed. 'Rob, I don't think your mother's a bad woman. We just didn't hit it off, we both made harsh judgements about each other and it's going to take some time to heal the wounds on both sides.'

'I know. Thank you for trying. I do realise she isn't always easy.'

That surprised her, and maybe it was why she let her guard down, because after that they moved on and Rob asked her about her photography, how she'd got into it, how many weddings a year she did, how many she turned down.

'Lots,' she told him. 'My real job's with the paper, doing my weekly column and features for them. I call it my jobby—sort of a cross between a job and a hobby. I mean, it is a job, and I make sure I treat it as one, being professional and doing things on time and not letting people down, but on the other hand it's my passion, my love, and it really is a hobby. It's had to be, because of Jenni. I would have been a photographer—that was the way I was going at college, with the journalism thing. But life as a female photo-journalist is a tough one, and it's not suited to motherhood, and I'm not sure it's really suited to me.'

'So you turned to weddings.'

'Not for years. I did some photography with my newspaper job as part of my features writing, but then someone asked me to do their wedding because they'd lost their photographer, and I stepped in to help them out. And then another friend of theirs saw them and asked me, and it sort of grew from there. It's great fun, and it tops up what I earn from the paper so I can have a few luxuries and do a bit to the house.'

He swirled his glass again, watching the wine intently, then set it down, very slowly and deliberately.

'Talk to me about the house,' he said quietly. 'I can't believe you still think of it as mine. It's yours, and you should be doing things to it—the French doors, for instance. That was why I put it in your name, so you could do what you wanted with it, but you haven't.'

She tried to smile, but it was hard with him being so obviously troubled by her admission. Instead she reached out a hand and laid it over his, the one that wasn't now carefully pushing a few crumbs into a neat, orderly row.

'I haven't been unhappy there, Rob,' she told him softly. 'It's been a great house in many ways—handy for everything, lovely for Jenni growing, a good school—I couldn't have wanted more, so it would have been ludicrous to move. And to be fair, I haven't had the money for wholesale alterations.'

'You wouldn't take it.'

'I didn't need your money, Rob. I was fine. I had the house. That was more than enough.'

His hand turned over, enclosing hers in its warmth. 'But you don't feel as if it's yours.'

No, she wanted to tell him, I feel as if it should be *our* house, as if you have a place there, will always have a place there. But of course she couldn't. 'Ignore me,' she advised. 'I was just being silly.'

'Because you didn't want me to stay.'

It wasn't a question, and she sighed. 'It's—'

She broke off and he put in, 'Difficult?'

She nodded. 'Yes. There just seems to be so much going on under the surface, so much we haven't talked about, so much that we've left undisturbed for so long that we can't even remember it, but it's still there, simmering away under a huge pile of dust. And if we disturb it...'

His thumb stroked idly over the backs of her fingers, testing the softness of her skin. 'Maybe we need to open the windows and blow the dust away, Maisie,' he said, totally forgetting his earlier decision to leave it alone, at least until after the wedding. 'Get everything out into the open. Talk about the things we haven't talked about.'

'Such as?'

He gave a soft laugh and sat back, releasing her hand before he gave in to the urge to press his lips to that soft, smooth palm. 'Well, if I knew that, I'd be halfway there,' he said, his mouth tilted in a wry half-smile. 'Look, forget it. I don't want to make you uncomfortable. I'll stay at a hotel.'

'Don't be silly. Your things are all there now, it's pointless. Anyway, I can always lock my bedroom door.'

Why, oh, why had she said that? His head came up and he speared her with those extraordinary slate-blue eyes. In the candlelight—how had she known the place had had a makeover and gone romantic?—they seemed to glint with fire, and he shook his head slowly.

'You don't need to lock your door. All you need to do—all you've ever needed to do—is say no to me.'

'Well, that's the problem, isn't it?' she said without thinking. 'I don't seem to be able to.'

His eyes became shuttered, and he leant back a little further. 'You used to manage it. After Jenni was born, the hatches were well and truly battened down.'

She let out a small, shocked breath and looked away. 'That was different. I was—I don't know. Afraid. You'd been away, the birth had traumatised me in all sorts of ways—I wasn't really myself. And you seemed different, too. Indifferent, even.'

'Indifferent? Maisie, I was never indifferent! I was trying to give you space.'

'Really?' She gave a tiny huff of laughter, and rubbed her arms, suddenly cold. 'It didn't feel like it. It felt like you couldn't bear to be in the same room as me.'

'I was afraid to touch you,' he admitted, his voice low as he leant towards her again, his eyes troubled. 'Afraid I might hurt you. Mrs McCrae had taken me on one side and made it clear that you'd had a dreadful time. I had no idea what that might even mean—'

'You never asked.'

'No,' he said, after a long pause. 'No, I didn't. I didn't know how to.'

'You could have just held me. Hugged me. Taken me to bed and held me in your arms all night—except, of course, after I had Jenni, you didn't seem to want to know. And when I was feeding her, you avoided me like the plague.'

'I didn't want to embarrass you.'

She laughed, staring at him in disbelief, and then realised he was serious. 'Rob, you were her *father*,' she said softly. 'You knew my body like your own, and I knew yours. Why would I be embarrassed? I thought *you* were embarrassed.'

He gave a low, tired laugh and looked up, catching the waiter's eye. 'Let's get out of here,' he said. 'I need some air.'

They left the restaurant and walked slowly back along the river, pausing by the spot where they'd picnicked earlier, and he turned to her, taking her hands in his, staring down into her eyes. His were shadowed so she couldn't read them, but his mouth was unsmiling, almost sad.

'Maisie, I'm sorry. If I could turn the clock back, I would, but I can't, and we're stuck with where we are now. And, really, I'm not sure anything's any different, is it? We still don't know each other. We still live at opposite ends of the country. Maybe we should leave the dust alone.'

'Maybe we should,' she agreed, but as she said it, she felt tears well in her eyes. They were laying their love to rest, but it had never died, just starved and withered as surely as if it had been flung into the dungeon at the castle, and just like the smell of food drifting through the slit high in the wall to torment those early prisoners, there had been the bitter-sweet, constant reminders of Rob over the years—phone calls and visits to Jenni, discussions about matters concerning her, every birthday and Christmas a disappointment for one or other of them. The wedding was just another one, more bitter-sweet than any other, and after the wedding would come grandchildren—christenings, Christmas, more birthdays, more babies. More reminders of all she'd lost.

She freed her hands and turned away, heading blindly back towards the house, and he followed her, a step behind, in silence.

'Coffee?' she asked as they went in, trying to be civilised, but he shook his head.

'No. I think I'll turn in. I've got a long drive tomorrow.'

'You haven't given me the wedding invitations yet.'

'No. I'll do that now. There's a disk with all the names and addresses on, so you should be able to print labels from it to save you writing them by hand.'

'There aren't that many, are there? I might do it now, and you can take the Scottish ones with you.'

'There are all the inserts to fold.'

She glanced at her watch. 'Rob, it's only ten. Unless you've changed your habits drastically, you never go to bed before midnight. We could make a start on it together. I can fold, you can write, because your writing's better than mine.'

'It's illegible.'

That was true. It was interesting, individual, but you had to know it to understand it.

'OK, you fold, I'll write,' she said. 'I'll put the kettle on. Or you can go to bed and I'll do it on my own.'

'I thought you wanted me out of your hair?'

'Not so badly that I want to do the invitations on my own.'

He smiled at that, and went to get them while she boiled the kettle.

'Tea or coffee? Or do you want something alcoholic?'

'Coffee,' he said, resigned to a long and sleepless night anyway, and thinking that a clear head might not be a bad idea, to stop him getting up and breaking down her door.

By the time she brought it through to the dining room-cum-study, he'd spread the stationery out in piles on the table, so that she could be writing the names on the envelopes and invitations while he collated and folded the other bits.

'Right, let's see this list,' she said, settling down beside him so that her warm, delicate scent drifted across to him and tunnelled ruthlessly under the hatches of his self-control.

He pulled it up on his little notebook computer, propped it in front of her and turned his attention to folding.

'Wow. Finally!' she said, handing him the Scottish stack. 'Stamps?'

'Of course.' He pulled a sheet of stamps out, and they stuck them on their separate piles, then he looked up and met her eyes. 'Thanks.'

'No, thank you. I did offer, and you ended up doing it anyway.'

'Consider it penance for all my endless failings.'

'I don't think you had any more failings than me,' she said quietly, picking up the tray and taking it back to the kitchen. He followed her, propping himself up and watching as she put the mugs in the dishwasher and rinsed out the cafetière and turned it upside down. Then she wiped her hands, turned back to him and raised a brow. 'More coffee? Or tea?'

He shook his head. 'No. I really do need to try and get some sleep, I've got six hundred miles to drive in the morning.'

She nodded, rubbing her arms briskly with her hands, making her breasts jiggle slightly. 'Right. I'm going to turn in, too. Do you want to take the bathroom first? I've got one or two things to do down here.'

'Sure. Thanks.'

He washed quickly, trying to get out of her way before she came up, but he was too slow. She was there, sitting on the edge of her bed—his bed, he realised in surprise. He recognised the old black iron frame that he'd brought from home, and it brought memories crashing back over him. Memories of Maisie trailing her hair over his chest, while he lay on his back, teeth clenched, gripping the rails of the headboard while she teased him. Memories of lying with her in the lazy aftermath of their love-making.

Memories of the first time he'd made love to her...

'I'm finished in the bathroom,' he said, and she looked up and smiled.

'Thanks. I'll see you in the morning.'

It was a clear dismissal, but he didn't take it. Instead he stepped into the room, running his hand over one of the big brass knobs on the foot of the bed.

'I didn't realise you'd still got this,' he said, his voice sounding a little taut and uneven to his ears.

'Yes. There didn't seem to be any point in getting rid of it. I changed the mattress a few years ago.'

'Of course.'

Her eyes were wary, huge in her pale face. He ought to leave, to go to his room and lock the door and push the key under it so he couldn't let himself out. Instead he reached out his hand, his fingers cool from the brass, and trailed them over her warm, smooth cheek.

'You're still beautiful, Maisie,' he said softly.

'Rob…'

He dropped his hand and took a step back. 'No. You're right. It would be foolish, wouldn't it?' he murmured. And anyway, he'd promised her, told her that all she'd ever needed to do was say no. Well, she was saying it now, and he had to respect that, had to walk away.

But she stood up, and he just had to taste her, had to kiss her. Nothing more. Just a kiss goodnight.

He bent his head, his lips brushing hers lightly before settling, and with a tiny sigh she lifted her hands to his shoulders and laid them there. To push him away, or draw him closer?

She did neither, just stood there while their mouths clung, the softest, lightest, most chaste kiss imaginable.

And then he eased away. His chest was taut, his heart racing, and he was within a hair of tearing off that wretched dress that hid her from his desperate, hungry eyes.

So he took a step back, and then another, reaching the door and hanging onto it as if it would help to hold him back.

'Goodnight, Maisie,' he said gruffly, and turning on his heel he crossed the little landing in a stride and went into his daughter's room and closed the door.

Firmly.

CHAPTER EIGHT

HE was gone by the time she woke in the morning.

She went down to the kitchen, hearing the sound of the washing machine spinning as she approached, and saw a note propped against the kettle.

'Sheets in washer. Thanks for yesterday, and doing invitations. See you soon, Rob.'

Thanks for yesterday.

Which part of it? The picnic on the river? Putting him in touch with Annette? Dinner?

The kiss?

Her breath hitched in her chest, and she stared down at the blur of sheets in the machine and felt a pang of regret that he'd done that, that he hadn't left the task to her, so she could have stripped them off and carried them downstairs with her nose pressed to the soft cotton, inhaling the scent of him.

She was being *ridiculous*! Thank goodness he'd done it for her, because her fevered imagination didn't need any more fuel to fan the flames. She'd spent most of last night lying awake thinking of him in the bed next door, just the thickness of a wall away, her body aching for another kiss, another touch.

More than that. Too much more. Dangerously, insanely too much more.

She'd fallen asleep at last, and had missed him leaving. The washing machine must have woken her—it had a tendency to thump when it started spinning. So he'd been gone—what? An hour and a half? So he must have left at five.

She wondered how much sleep he'd had, or if he'd given up and headed off, intending to book into a hotel en route and get a few more hours.

She turned the kettle on and picked up his note. She needed to stop thinking about him sleeping, because sleeping meant bed, and bed meant trouble. Big trouble.

She didn't need any more trouble than she was already in. Dinner last night had been like a drug, sitting with him in a candlelit restaurant, walking by the river—foolish. And he wanted her to go to the hotel in Ardnashiel for a food tasting and go through that all over again?

Including the kiss goodnight?

A shiver of what could have been excitement ran over her skin, and she crushed it ruthlessly. He hadn't meant anything by it. She was reading things where there were none. If he'd wanted to, he could so easily have made love to her last night. She hadn't resisted, but she hadn't allowed herself to beg either, and given free rein, he'd walked away.

He'd probably slept like a log, she told herself in disgust, and making a cup of tea she took it into the study and tackled the accounts that were waiting for her attention.

They were getting busy on the estate, spring giving way to summer and the tourist season getting under way, so there was plenty to keep Rob occupied when he got back.

He was glad of that. Alec was working hard, but it was just as well because it left Jenni free to concentrate on her studies, and in any of his free time he was decorating the gatehouse, ready for them to move in straight after the wedding.

That left Rob, of course, in between a million and one admin jobs at Ardnashiel and juggling his business in London, to sort the rest of the wedding details, and because he didn't want to trouble Jenni, and because he trusted Maisie's judgement more than his mother's on the subject of contemporary weddings, inevitably he'd end up talking more to her.

It would be hard.

Not as hard as lying there all night beside her, with just the wall between them, so he could reach out and lay his hand on it and feel closer to her. That had been hell, and he'd given up and left when it had became obvious that he was going to get no sleep that night.

He'd pulled over in a service area and reclined his seat so that he could doze for a while, but he'd been glad to get home and go to bed for ten hours of solid, uninterrupted sleep, and when he'd woken up, he'd given himself a serious talking-to and moved on.

No more dreaming about what might have been, no more longing for things he couldn't and was never going to have, no more turning the clock back. He was living in the here and now, and here and now he was rushed off his feet.

But the problems kept coming to find him anyway, starting with the florist.

She had a problem, apparently, so he discovered ten days after he'd got back. Jenni wanted flowers over the arched doorway at the entrance to the church, but the florist didn't know either how to fix them or what, exactly, was required. What about pew ends? Pedestals? And how many tables would there be? And what were the bride's mother and the groom's mother going to require in the way of corsages?

How the hell was he supposed to know? It was a minefield.

He went and studied the church doorway, and discovered that at some point someone had inserted small rings around the top of the arch—for decorating it?

Whatever they'd been for, they were there, so he could tick that box.

As for what Jenni had planned to be fixed there, he was lost—never mind the number of tables and the corsages and all the other stuff.

So he phoned Maisie, and the sound of her slightly distracted voice went straight to his gut and tied it in knots.

'Hi. Florist questions,' he said, getting straight to the point. 'Have you got time to talk?'

'Um—yes, sure. Sorry. I was just editing a feature. Actually, can I call you back? I need to email it now.'

'Sure.'

He hung up, made himself a coffee and paced around his office until the phone rang. Stupidly, it made him jump, and his heart raced.

Unnecessarily. It was the hotel. Had they decided yet on the menu?

'No. I'll call you—we need to have another tasting.'

'Would you like to book it?'

'I can't,' he told her, 'not right now. I might be able to in about half an hour—can I call you?'

'Of course.'

He hung up, and the phone rang again almost immediately. 'Hi.'

'It's the hotel again, Mr Mackenzie. I forgot to say we can't do any tastings on Friday or Saturday nights now, because the hotel's full on those nights for the next several weeks, so it would be best to go for midweek, if you can.'

'Fine.' It meant Jenni couldn't be there, but that was fine. He was happy to go on his own with Maisie. More than happy.

He hung up again, drummed his fingers, made another coffee—and then she rang.

'Rob, hi, I'm sorry it took so long,' she said apologetically, her voice soft and lyrical. Damn. His guts were knotted again.

'That's fine,' he said. 'I've been busy with other calls.'

Well, it wasn't really a lie. 'The florist wants to know what you want over the church door—we've solved the fixing problem, there are rings up there, but she's not sure—she was talking pedestals and garlands and pew thingamies—she just lost me.'

Maisie chuckled. 'It's OK, I know exactly. Give me her email address, I'll send her some photos. What else?'

'Table centres—how many tall, how many low? How many, generally, but we haven't had all the replies yet so I can't tell her. Oh, and what are you and Alec's mother wearing, and what do you want as a corsage?'

'I don't know about Alec's mother, you'll have to ask her. It needs to be something to tone with the other flowers. And does your mother want one? She might well. You'd better ask her, too.'

'OK. And you?'

He could hear her fractional hesitation, sense her reluctance.

'I'm not sure,' she said, surprising him. 'I'm having second thoughts about my outfit.'

'But I thought that was all settled? You bought it when you were with Jenni. She wouldn't tell me anything about it, though, just told me I had to wait and see. She wouldn't even tell me the colour, never mind what it looked like. She just said I'd like it.'

There was a muffled sound at the other end. 'Um—it's cream,' she said after a pause. 'Like really rich clotted cream—and it's lace.'

'Cream? I thought only the bride should wear white or cream?' he queried, struggling with the etiquette.

'It's up to the bride, and anyway, it's a rich cream, almost gold. And Jenni loved it, she told me I had to have it, but…'

'What? You don't sound too sure,' he said, leaning back and propping his feet up on the desk. 'If you're not certain, get something else. I know Jenni approved it, but you shouldn't let that influence you if you don't feel good in it.'

'Oh, I feel good in it. I love it.'

That confused him completely. 'So what's the problem?' he asked, wondering how something so straightforward could be so hard. 'Doesn't it fit?'

'Yes, but—that's the trouble, really.' He could almost hear her chewing her lip. 'I'm just not sure. It's very…fitted.'

He felt the heat ramp up a few degrees. 'Fitted?' he said, his throat suddenly tight.

'Yes—it's sort of snug, and it tucks in under the bottom and just…well, it fits. It fits beautifully. I'm just not sure it's—I don't know, motherly enough.'

It didn't sound in the least bit motherly. He was going to choke if he couldn't breathe soon, and his entire body was on red alert. 'I'm sure it'll be lovely. Jenni liked it,' he reminded her, desperate now to see this dress that tucked in under her cute, delectable bottom that just fitted so well in his hands.

'Look, it doesn't matter. It's a lovely outfit, and at the end of the day if I go for something that tones with cream it'll go with whatever I end up wearing, if it's not that. I'll talk to the florist. Was there anything else?'

Was there?

'Ah—yes. Food tasting. When can you come up? It's Jenni's twenty-first in a fortnight, and she's coming home for the weekend. She's out with her friends on Friday night, and then coming up on Saturday morning, so you'll probably want to be here, won't you, for that?'

'Oh. Yes, of course. Um…I've made sure I'm free that weekend, and I've got time before and after to allow for travelling.'

'So why not come before? We can't do the food tasting at the weekend, because they're too busy, but they can do midweek. How about coming up overnight on Tuesday, and we'll go on Wednesday evening. Then you can see the florist and sort out any other details and go back the following week.'

There was a small silence, and then a quiet sigh. 'OK. I'll do that.'

'I'll book it,' he said, quickly, before she could change her mind. 'I'll email you the booking reference and the florist's email address so you can send her the pictures and arrange for her to come to the castle and the church and see what we're talking about, and I'll see you next week.'

He hung up before she could argue, dropped his feet to the floor and sucked in a deep breath. All he could see was Maisie's firm, rounded bottom lovingly snuggled in rich, creamy lace, and it was doing his head in.

He booked the sleeper, emailed her all the details he'd promised and went out for a long, hard walk.

With only four weeks to go to the wedding, Maisie went to see Jeff and spoke to him in more detail about the photos.

'I'm going up in a couple of days,' she told him, 'and I'll take some more shots of the church, the castle, the grounds—just so you know what you're dealing with. There's a disk here with lots on already, and I've labelled them so you know what they all are, but you could do with finding your way around beforehand. When will you be able to get there?'

He shrugged, relaxed and certain of himself. 'Maisie, I'll do whatever you tell me to do. When do you want me there?'

'By the Friday morning at the latest? You can see the marquee, work out what shots you want, talk to Jenni and Alec about what they want, then in the morning you can take photos of Jenni getting ready, and walk down with us to the church.'

'What if it rains? Will there be a car?'

'On standby.' She looked him in the eye. 'It won't rain. It's not allowed to rain.' And then she sighed. 'It's Scotland. Of course it'll rain. Oh, damn, Jeff, why is it all so complicated?' she asked him, and he gave a soft chuckle and made her a coffee.

'Chill. It'll be fine. It'll be a lovely, sunny day, and even if it's not, I'll get you some brilliant atmospheric umbrella shots. You'll have a great time.'

He was right, of course. She'd been to lots of wet weddings, and the weather had never put more than a fleeting dampener on the party spirits. She was just used to East Anglia, where the sun shone more often.

'I'll do whatever you want. It's your girl's day, not mine, and you know what you're aiming for. And trust me.'

'I do trust you. I wouldn't ask anyone else. You're a darling,' she told him with a smile, kissed his designer-stubbled cheek and sat back with her coffee and chilled, just like he'd told her to. He was right, she could trust him. He'd do just what she asked, and he'd do it well.

She gave an inward sigh of relief, ticked that box and scanned her mental list.

Accessories. She still hadn't chosen shoes or bag—still hadn't reconciled herself to the outfit, come to that, never mind worked out if she wanted a hat. She finished her coffee, then went home and pulled the outfit out of the wardrobe and put it on.

And swallowed. It really did hug her body lovingly. Very lovingly.

Oh, it was elegant enough, and beautifully, superbly cut. And it definitely suited her.

It'll knock Dad's socks off.

Her heart gave a little lurch, and she pressed her hand to her chest and breathed in. Silly. She put the bolero on, hoping it would make it more demure, but the peep of skin through the lace was somehow more alluring, more sensual.

But she did love it. She turned round, held a mirror up and studied her posterior critically, and then threw the mirror down with a sigh. To hell with Rob. She loved it, she wanted to wear it and he'd probably be too worried about his speech to notice her.

She took it off, put it in a bag and went shopping for accessories.

He wasn't at the station to meet her. Instead of Rob, she found Helen on the platform, looking a little wary.

'Maisie—welcome back,' she said with a tentative smile. 'Did you have a good journey?'

She nodded. 'It was fine. I never sleep very well on the train, but it was fine. I take it Rob's busy?'

'Yes. He's out on the hills with some guests. Alec had to sort something out for the gatehouse, so I offered to come and get you. I hope you don't mind.'

Maisie smiled, reached over and hugged her.

'Of course I don't mind. In fact, if you're not in a hurry, why don't we have coffee at that lovely place on the way?'

'Oh. Well, that would be very nice,' she agreed, returning the smile less tentatively. 'Actually, I could do with your advice,' she admitted. 'I'm not sure about my outfit for the wedding.'

Maisie laughed, picked up her case and followed Helen to the car. 'You as well?' she said, and Helen looked at her in puzzlement. 'I wasn't sure about my dress. Jenni loves it, but…'

'Jenni said you look wonderful in it. She said the colouring was perfect for you, and it was the most beautiful fit.'

'It is. I'm just not sure it's motherly enough,' she said, repeating the words she'd said to Rob earlier, but Helen flapped her hand.

'Do people really worry about that sort of thing these days? I have a philosophy. If it makes you feel good, wear it, if it doesn't, don't, and it doesn't matter what it is. I try not to dress inappropriately, but I do always insist on being me, and it's always stood me in good stead. The thing is, do you feel like you, or like someone else dressed up?'

She thought about that as she loaded her case into the boot and got in the car. 'Me,' she said after a pause. 'I feel like me—but different. Better.'

'Then it's right,' Helen said. 'The trouble with mine is I feel like me, but old and stuffy and tedious rather than better.'

'Is it a new outfit?' Maisie asked, happy to keep the conversation on safe ground, and Helen told her about it, that it was on approval and could be exchanged, that she'd tried several things but not known which to go for.

'I don't suppose you could spare the time while you're up here to help me choose something else, could you?' she asked tentatively, and Maisie was surprised, yet again, at her reticence. She'd remembered her as matriarchal and rather bossy, but this woman was uncertain, almost conciliatory. Had Rob given her a hard time for being mean? Was that it? Was Helen trying to make amends for all the bitterness and unhappiness around the time of Jenni's birth?

'Of course I can spare the time,' she said. 'It'll be a pleasure.'

Helen's face lit up, and she pulled up in the car park of the lochside café a few moments later still smiling, and turned to Maisie. 'Well, here we are. Shall we go in?'

They found a table by the window—the table she'd sat at with Rob when they'd had their revealing and painful conversation—and she vowed that this time she'd guard her tongue and try incredibly hard not to fall out with his mother. She was being nice today, but Maisie was under no illusions. It was a fragile truce—or so she thought, until they were seated and the waitress had taken their order.

Then her smile faltered briefly, and she met Maisie's eyes, her own clouded. 'Maisie, I—I owe you such an apology. I've treated you badly in the past, and I'm so ashamed of what I did. I didn't know you, I didn't try and get to know you, or give you the benefit of the doubt, and I think I misjudged you terribly. I thought you were using Rob for your own ends, and I had no idea—well, that you'd been so innocent. I really thought you were just after his wealth.'

Maisie gave a soft laugh. 'Helen, I didn't even know he had any when I met him. I knew the house in Cambridge was his to live in, but I thought it was on a lease and he just wanted someone living there for security while he was away. I didn't know anything about housing then, I was still living at home. It didn't occur to me that he owned it. To be honest, it was such a gift I didn't look at it as closely as I should have done,' she admitted with a soft laugh. 'All I could think about was getting away from home, from a father who wouldn't let me wear make-up and a brother who thought I'd been put on earth to take over where my mother left off. Only, of course, once

I was pregnant neither of them wanted anything to do with me, my father because I'd brought shame on my mother's name, my brother because the last thing he wanted was a screaming brat in the house.'

Helen clucked softly, and shook her head. 'I had no idea. When Rob moved you up here to have Jenni, so you wouldn't be alone, I had no idea that you would have been quite *so* alone. And—well, we didn't exactly make you welcome, did we?'

Maisie shook her head ruefully. 'Not exactly. But looking at it from your point of view, would I have acted any differently? I don't know that I would.'

Helen gave a strained little smile. 'It's very generous of you to say that, Maisie, but I think you would, you know. You don't have it in you to be harsh or judgemental.'

Maisie laughed at that. 'Oh, Helen, you're so wrong,' she said, her voice filled with regret. 'I thought you were stuck-up and cold-hearted, and I was convinced you hated me and thought I wasn't good enough for your son.'

'I did,' she said honestly. 'But I didn't know you, my dear. And you've done a wonderful job of raising your daughter. It's just such a pity that you and Rob weren't together to do it.'

She sighed. 'Yes. He's missed a lot.'

'He's missed *you*,' Helen said softly, surprising her. Maisie gave a tiny gasp of laughter and shook her head.

'No. No, he hasn't. After he came back from the navy, he was different. He wasn't interested in me. Jenni, yes. He adored her. Me? I'm not convinced he thought of me as anything other than the mother of his child.'

'I think you're wrong. I think he really loved you, and I think he still does.'

Her head flew up, her eyes meeting Helen's in disbelief. 'No,' she whispered.

Helen nodded, and Maisie turned her head and stared out over the water. Rob still love her? He could hardly be in the same room with her without them arguing.

But he'd kissed her—so softly, so tenderly.

And then he'd walked away.

Was that the act of a man in love? She didn't think so. A man in love would have stayed, taken what she was so freely, so willingly offering. Or would he? Would he have walked away, and hoped that she'd follow in her own time?

As she had with him?

Suddenly she couldn't wait to see him, didn't want to sit there with Helen talking about him, but wanted to be with him, to talk to him, to see if there might be any truth in his mother's words.

But he was out walking over the hills with some

guests, so there was no hurry. She forced herself to drink the coffee their waitress put down in front of her at that moment, and she switched the conversation from Rob to Jenni, to the wedding, to Alec and how the gatehouse was coming on—anything rather than speculate on whether the man she loved still cared about her as anything other than the mother of his daughter…

He couldn't wait to see her.

He would have been there to meet her, but Alec had had a hitch with the kitchen fitters and he'd had to take the guided walk out instead.

He just hoped his mother wasn't causing a riot with Maisie. He didn't think she would, but he couldn't be sure, and he was on tenterhooks for the entire day. They got back at four-thirty, and the guests headed off to their cottage with effusive thanks and he took the dogs in through the kitchen door and found Maisie sitting there with Mrs McCrae, dribbling what looked suspiciously like his best brandy into the bottom of a massive fruit cake.

'Don't tell me—the wedding cake?' he asked, kissing Mrs McCrae on the cheek and earning a swat on the shoulder for his pains, and then he met Maisie's eyes and his heart turned over.

How could the woman grow more lovely every time he saw her? 'Hi, there. Good journey?' he asked, leaning over to brush his lips against her cheek, relishing the softness, breathing in the scent of her and stifling a groan.

'Pretty much as predicted. How was your guided walk?'

'Pretty much as predicted,' he said with a chuckle. 'I'm starving, Mrs M. Any sticky ginger-bread left?'

'You know fine well there's not, you finished it yesterday. There's shortbread cooling on the rack, and tea in the pot. And Alec said thanks, and the kitchen's going to be done on time.'

'Really? I wonder what he threatened them with?' he said mildly, breaking off a chunk of shortbread and pouring himself a mug of tea while he munched it.

'I hope you're not going to eat so much you aren't ready for this food tasting?' Maisie said, eyeing the shortbread.

'Not a chance,' he said round a mouthful. 'I'm ravenous. I've probably walked nearly twenty miles today. I'm going to make a few phone calls, and then I'm getting into the bath. I'll see you later, Maisie. Six-thirty OK for you? Our reservation's at seven.'

'Six-thirty's fine,' she said, so with a brisk nod, he grabbed another chunk of shortbread and headed for the stairs, then stuck his head back into the kitchen.

'Don't wear stilts, by the way, we're walking down as it's fine so we can check out all the wines.'

'OK. Dress code?'

'Pretty.'

'That doesn't sound like a dress code,' she pointed out, but then had to watch his mouth twitch into a mischievous grin.

'It's my dress code,' he murmured. 'See you in a couple of hours.'

And with a wicked wink he was gone, leaving her sitting there, her heart drumming, her mouth slightly open.

She shut it, fast, but not so fast that Mrs McCrae didn't notice, and she felt her cheeks burn.

'Shall I wrap the cake again now?' she asked hastily, and without waiting for an answer she closed the greaseproof paper round it and put the lid back on.

The hotel restaurant was busy, even though it was midweek, and Rob was interested to see how many of their own guests were eating there.

No wonder the owner was giving them such a good deal on the wedding breakfast! Clearly their business brought in a lot of trade, but the disadvantage was the lack of privacy. He was recognised, of course, and he didn't want to be. He wanted this to be about them—about the food, too, of course, because of the wedding, but mostly about them, because with every day that passed he grew more uncertain about the reasons for their divorce.

'It's lovely in here,' Maisie said, looking around the restaurant. Modern tables and chairs, slate table mats, and above all the view over the sea from the floor-to-ceiling windows made it a wonderful place to eat, and it didn't hurt that the food was excellent, he thought.

They were shown to a quiet table, tucked out of the way in an alcove but still with a stunning view across the sea to the islands. 'I'll tell the chef you're here,' the waiter said, disappearing, and moments later he arrived, smiling and greeting Maisie enthusiastically.

'So like Jenni. I would have known at once who you were. OK, the menu. You were undecided, Mr Mackenzie?'

He dragged his eyes back off Maisie and looked at the chef. 'Yes. They liked the duck and the chicken. I wondered about that. I thought maybe the lamb would be better, or change the starter to something else—scallops, perhaps.'

'I shall cook you one of everything, and let you share—would that be the best idea? And then you can choose. And wine—I'll bring you a bottle of each, red and white, to get a balance.'

He disappeared, leaving them alone, and suddenly the small alcove seemed airless to Maisie.

'So, how was the journey really?' Rob asked softly, and she laughed.

'Oh, it was all right. I'm getting used to it, I've done it a few times now, and it's long and tedious, but it's less stressful than flying with all the parking problems and hanging around for check-in. Still, next time I come up will be the last for a while, I expect.'

Something flickered briefly in his eyes and was gone, and she forced herself to be business-like. 'So—I'm seeing the florist tomorrow?'

'Yes. She's coming at nine. I've cleared my diary. I didn't know if you'd need me, but I'll be about if so.'

Need him? Oh, yes, she needed him, but not in the way he meant.

'Thanks.' She twirled her empty wineglass absently, then set it down. 'So, what else has been going on, wedding-wise?'

'No. I don't want to talk about it. Let's talk about something else.'

She met his eyes and smiled in relief. 'Do you know what? I'd love to talk about something else. Why don't you tell me about your day?'

He shrugged slowly. 'Not much to tell. I walked miles. It was good.'

'See any tourist eagles?'

He gave a soft chuckle, and tore a piece off his roll, shredding it bit by bit. 'No. No eagles of any sort. These rolls are lovely and soft. And warm. Interesting. What flavour's yours?'

'I don't know. It's got seeds in…mmm. Nice. How about yours?'

'Sundried tomato—here, try it,' he said, and held it up to her lips.

She leant back slightly and took it from his hand, but it didn't help because their fingers brushed anyway and it was nearly as potent. She chewed and swallowed. 'Oh, that's lovely.'

'Give me some of yours?'

No way. She pushed the plate towards him. 'Help yourself,' she said, and then to fill the silence she asked, 'How's Alec getting on? I still haven't seen their house.'

'I'll show it to you tomorrow, when the florist's gone. It's coming on well— Ah, here's the food.'

He sounded almost relieved, which was ridiculous as it had been his idea to feed each other. The waiter set down three plates on the table between them.

'Scallops with chorizo, lemon and thyme on wild rocket, pan-fried oriental duck breast on summer leaves, and charred peppers with roasted goats' cheese and chilli oil dressing. Enjoy your meal.'

The sommelier arrived and poured a selection of wines, then left them to it, and Rob picked up his knife and fork, speared a piece of tender, succulent scallop with a sliver of crisp, spicy sausage and held it to her lips. 'Try this. It gets my vote every time,' he said, his voice soft and yet roughened, somehow, so that it teased at her senses.

She opened her mouth, took the morsel and closed her eyes, because she simply couldn't look at him a second longer. The flavour exploded on her tongue, and after a moment she opened her eyes again and nodded.

'That's lovely.'

'Isn't it? Here, try the duck.'

She stabbed it herself, then moved on to the pepper and goats' cheese. 'Let me try that,' he murmured, and with her heart pumping she put a little on her fork and held it out to him, watching spellbound as his firm, full lips closed around the fork and he drew it off and chewed, slowly and thoughtfully.

'No. OK for the veggies, but the goats' cheese doesn't do it for me. Try the scallop again.'

And once again his fork was at her lips, his eyes locked with hers, and the air between them was brittle with tension.

She didn't know how she got through the meal. He fed her chicken breast stuffed with Brie and wrapped in Parma ham, served on a bed of haggis—haggis, of all things, but as he said, it was a Scottish wedding—and rack of lamb on neeps and tatties—again the Scottish thing—with a red-currant and rosemary *jus*.

'I like the chicken,' she said, struggling with the whole feeding bit, because he would insist on mixing flavours and offering them to her, a bit from one plate with a bit from another, just to see if the dishes needed adjusting. 'What about the vegetarians?'

'They're having wild mushroom risotto with some pesto something-or-other. I don't know. Jenni liked it. What do you think of the wines?'

'I like the white. I'm not much of a red wine drinker but it's beautifully smooth.'

'I think so. Ready to try the desserts?'

'I think so, but really only a little,' she said. The dessert had been pretty much unanimously agreed, an *assiette* of lemon tart, chocolate mousse and vanilla ice cream in a tiny brandy snap basket. It was beautifully presented, but Rob had asked for just one to share, so this was worse. This was him feeding her tasty chocolate mousse, as light as air and rich as Croesus, on the tip of a spoon—a spoon which had been in his mouth.

'How's the ice cream?' he asked, and opened

his mouth, a smile playing round his eyes as he waited for her to return the favour.

Outwardly, they were doing nothing but sharing their desserts. Inwardly—inwardly, he was causing havoc, and when they'd scraped up the last morsel of creamy deliciousness and the waiter suggested coffee, she shook her head.

'No, thank you, I'm fine. I don't need anything more.' Because there would be truffles, and he'd insist on holding one to her lips, or biting one in half and feeding her the rest, and she didn't think she could stand it.

'I agree,' he said, and moments later the chef appeared at their side.

'So, how did you get on?' he asked.

'Excellent,' Rob said warmly. 'A really great meal. And I think we're agreed on the scallops, the chicken and the *assiette*.'

'Excellent choice. Well, we're looking forward to cooking it for you on the wedding day. Fingers crossed for the weather.'

'You do that,' Maisie said with a smile as she got to her feet. Heavens, she felt a tiny bit tipsy. All that wine tasting, she thought, and when the fresh air hit her, she felt suddenly light-headed.

'Are you all right?'

'Yes—a bit tired. I'll be all right after I've had some sleep. I can't sleep properly on the train.'

And the alcohol might have left her system by then. Not that she'd had much, but she didn't drink, as a rule, and any was more than usual.

'It's very dark.'

'It's all right. Here, give me your hand,' he said, and tucked it into the crook of his arm, his fingers wrapped over hers as they walked slowly back up the hill from the village.

'I can't believe our little girl's going to be married and living there in just four weeks,' she said as they passed the gatehouse and walked down the drive over the stone bridge into the castle forecourt.

'I know. It only seems like yesterday she was a baby. I've been trying to write my speech, and there's so much I want to say, so much to remember. I don't want to leave any of it out.'

'Rather you than me. I'd hate to make a speech.'

He chuckled quietly and led her into the kitchen, then put the kettle on the stove and turned to lean against it, arms folded, his eyes strangely pensive.

'It's so good to have you back here,' he said softly. 'It feels somehow right, as if you're back where you belong.'

She opened her mouth to deny it, but no words came out. It *did* feel right, oddly. Almost as if there was a place for her here now, where there had never been a place for her before.

He shrugged away from the stove and moved slowly towards her, stopping when he was just inches away, lifting his hands and cupping her face tenderly in his palms. One thumb traced the edge of her lips, dragging slightly over the moist skin, bringing a whimper to her throat.

His eyes darkened and he lowered his head, touching his lips to hers, then with a ragged sigh he closed the gap and hauled her up against him, anchoring her head with one splayed hand while the other slid down and cupped her bottom, lifting her hard against him. She gave a little gasp, and he took instant advantage, his mouth plundering hers, the hot, moist sweep of his tongue dragging a ragged little cry from her heart.

It brought an echoing groan from deep inside him, and he lifted his head and stared down at her with wild, tortured eyes.

'Come to bed with me, Maisie,' he said softly, his voice roughened with a need so intense it made her legs buckle.

She closed her eyes, and felt a tear squeeze out from under one lid and slide slowly down her cheek. 'Oh, Rob, I can't. Don't ask that of me, please. It would be so easy, but we can't go there. Not now. I can't let you hurt me again, and you will, I know you will.'

'No! Maisie, no, I don't want to hurt you. I

never wanted to hurt you. It was just the wrong time for us.'

'And it's still the wrong time, Robert. It's still the wrong time. We've got a wedding to get through. I can't deal with this complication now.'

'And after the wedding? What then, my love?'

'I don't know,' she said, her voice little more than a whisper. 'Ask me then.'

And without waiting for his reply, she turned and walked out swiftly, running up the stairs to her room and closing the door firmly behind her. Then she turned the key, not to keep him out, because she knew he wouldn't follow her without invitation, but to keep herself in…

CHAPTER NINE

THE meeting with the florist went really well, to Maisie's relief, because by the following morning her nerves were stretched to breaking point and the last thing she needed was trouble with something so fundamental as Jenni's flowers, but the woman was as sensible and willing to listen in the flesh as she had been on the phone and in her emails.

She'd brought along a few ideas for table centres, a pew end, a photograph of a pedestal she'd done before that she thought might suit, and she promised to leave everything for Jenni to see on the weekend when she was coming home for her birthday.

They met up with Rob and Helen for coffee in the Great Hall, and Maisie was glad to have the two women there to act as a buffer between her and Rob.

As it was, when he passed her her coffee cup their fingers brushed and she nearly dropped the cup. 'Steady,' he murmured, his eyes gentle with understanding, as if telling her she had nothing to fear, he wasn't going to make it difficult.

He didn't need to. She was doing that all by herself.

She'd spent half the night glad she'd had the sense to walk away from him in the kitchen, and the other half regretting it. But now she was glad she'd walked away, because it had been the right thing to do, and she gave him a grateful little smile, took the cup and murmured, 'Thank you.'

'You're welcome,' he said, and they both knew they weren't talking about the coffee, but about some new understanding between them that had come out of nowhere, it seemed, an understanding that held her breathless with the promise of resolution of a love so long unfulfilled she'd almost forgotten what it felt like.

Really felt like, deep down inside her where her hopes and dreams had been locked up for so long she was afraid to open it up in case a chink of light would show them to be ashes. But they weren't ashes, they were glowing embers, just waiting for the chance to leap back to life.

She just hoped that in the fire that was sure to follow, she wouldn't get too badly burned…

The week of the wedding came upon them with the speed of light.

Maisie had gone back after the weekend of

Jenni's twenty-first birthday, a poignant day for both of them, and Rob had been glad in a way to see her go because the tension between them was palpable.

He missed her, though. Not that he had time to miss her, not really. He was working flat out at the castle, making sure that all the arrangements were in place and nothing had been left to chance, and he knew it would have been harder to concentrate on the detail with her there to distract him.

He remembered, somewhere in the dim and distant optimistic past, thinking that the worst was over once the planning had been done, and he remembered the guarded look in Maisie's eyes. She'd known, he thought with a wry laugh. Known what was to come, and let him keep his illusions a little bit longer.

He was aching to see her again. Two more days, he told himself. Just two more days. Jenni was home, complete with all her baggage from uni piled in heaps in one of the attic rooms, waiting for a calmer time to tackle the unpacking.

The gatehouse was almost ready, Alec having worked himself almost to a standstill to get it finished in time, and when he went over to see how they were getting on, he found them making up the bed with fresh, gleaming white linen.

'Isn't it lovely?' Jenni said, glowing with pride in Alec, and he thought how lucky they were. He swallowed a lump in his throat and nodded, avoiding looking at the bed.

Surely she wasn't old enough, his little girl. Not to feel the wild, tempestuous emotions he and Maisie were going through right now. The need so deep it was flaying him alive. The fear that it would all go wrong and he would lose more than he could ever have imagined.

'You've done a great job, Alec,' he said gruffly, and headed for the stairs, past the little room that might one day house his grandchild.

Grandchild! He wasn't in any way ready to be a grandfather, for heaven's sake! He was only just forty-three, still in his prime—or was he fooling himself?

'What's up, Pops?' Jenni slipped her arm into his and hugged it. 'Are you OK? You look sad.'

'End of an era,' he said quietly, turning her into his arms and hugging her. She tipped back her head and stared up at him.

'You aren't going to cry on Saturday, are you?' she said, and he gave a slightly strangled laugh.

'I don't plan to,' he said, knowing that the tears would be close to the surface for all that. So much emotion. And afterwards…

'I have to get on. I just wanted to see if you were both OK and if you needed anything else.'

'No. A bottle of milk, perhaps, for Sunday morning.'

Ah. Sunday morning, when they didn't realise they wouldn't be here, because he'd arranged a helicopter to whisk them away on their wedding night to a highly exclusive luxury retreat, away from all possible intrusions, to give their love the time and space it deserved to blossom.

'I think we might do better than just a pint of milk,' he said drily.

'Go on, then, push the boat out and buy us some croissants and bacon and eggs. Oh, and decent coffee. And smoked salmon. And champagne, if you're feeling flush!'

'Consider it done,' he teased, the smile easy to find because it was all arranged, and he had no doubt the room service there would provide for their every whim.

Libby and Tricia, her bridesmaids, were in on the secret and had promised to go through her clothes and pack a bag, and Alec's mother was doing the same for him.

All they had to do was get through the next few days…

Maisie didn't sleep on the train.

There were too many emotions, too much to do, too much of all of it, really. Excitement and nervous anticipation and little shivers of dread in case anything went wrong, and under it all, carefully controlled, a little quiver of hope.

He was there on the platform as the train pulled in, and he took her case from her, leaving her with the garment bag containing the dress and the hat box.

'Is that a hat box?' he said, eyeing it suspiciously, and she laughed.

'Don't worry, it's not huge. It's not even a real hat.'

'Not one of those stupid chicken things.'

She laughed again, so happy to see him, and shaking his head in denial, he dumped her case back down on the platform and hugged her.

'Oh, it's so good to see you,' he mumbled into her hair, and she turned her head and kissed his cheek.

'You, too.'

'I've missed you. It's really good to have you back.'

'It's good to be back,' she admitted, and he lifted his head and stared down at her, a quizzical frown on his face.

'Really?' he said softly, and she nodded.

'I never thought I'd say that, but it's true. It feels good to come—' She caught herself just in time, and said, 'Back.' Not home. Don't jump the gun, Maisie, she warned herself.

He picked up the case, slung his other arm

around her shoulders and ushered her through to the car park. He had a Range Rover today, and she raised an eyebrow. 'No sports car? On a lovely day like today?'

He grinned. 'I didn't know how much luggage you'd have,' he said, and slammed the boot shut, then opened the door for her. She climbed in, then turned her head, which was a mistake, because it was level with his and he leant in and touched his lips to hers.

Just that. Nothing else, no words, just a tender, fleeting kiss before he closed the door and went round to get in behind the wheel.

'No time for coffee today,' he told her as they headed out on the road. 'Jenni'll skin me alive if I keep you out too long, and the marquee people are there, so I ought to be at home.'

'I could have got a taxi,' she protested, but he threw her a smile that nearly melted her bones.

'No way. I wanted you to myself for a few minutes,' he told her, and she found her hand wrapped in his, trapped against the hard, solid warmth of his thigh. Just like before.

And just like before, they talked and laughed the whole way back to the castle. He told her about the honeymoon plans he'd made, and she told him about Annette and her progress.

'She's looking pretty tired, but they seem happy with her, and it's looking really positive.'

'Good. I'll have to go and see her again next time I'm down.'

Which implied she would be there, too, instead of here. So had she totally misread his intentions? Had he simply wanted to make love to her, nothing more, nothing less?

But he'd said he didn't want to hurt her, and he knew that would. So was he intending—?

She stopped herself. Now was not the time. She didn't have the emotional energy to concentrate on a love that had waited twenty years. It could wait another three or four days.

'So, tell me what's been going on. What's left to do?'

He laughed a little desperately, and said, 'Ah, yeah. Well—I have no idea. There's an endless list, but at least we're now down to the things that don't matter, rather than the things that do. Mrs McCrae and Alec's mother have polished the church within an inch of its life, the gatehouse is virtually ready, Alec's had his stag do—that was a bit of a laugh. They covered him in soot and treacle and feathers and dragged him through the village, and everyone came out and cheered him on. They all love him, and it was really touching to see it, but we had a bit of a game cleaning him up.'

'Poor Alec,' she murmured, smiling. 'How's his head?'

'Oh, just about recovered, I think. So's mine. Those boys know how to drink. I have no idea how much of my malt whisky they got through.'

Maisie turned and searched his eyes. 'You love him, don't you?'

'I do. He feels like a son to me, I have to say. It will be no hardship welcoming him to the family.'

'Oh, on which note, how's the speech coming on?'

He groaned, and she laughed and squeezed his hand. 'You'll be great. Don't worry.'

'I'm not worried about the speech. I'm worried I'll make a fool of myself. Jenni asked me if I was going to cry.'

'And will you?'

'I hope not.'

'I will.'

'Don't. You'll set me off.'

They exchanged smiles, and she felt a curious warmth curl around her heart. It was almost as if they were still married, still a couple, still Mum and Dad in the same breath, instead of with a comma and six hundred miles between them.

Except there was still the problem of the six hundred miles, she thought, and then realised, as they turned into the gates and rumbled slowly down the drive, it didn't seem like a problem any more, because suddenly the castle seemed like home. She just hoped the feeling lasted.

The morning of the wedding, to everyone's relief, was gloriously sunny, not a cloud in the sky, and Maisie sat in the window of her room and watched Rob walk the dogs along the beach and up to the old ruins on the headland. He stood there for a while, motionless, and then, as if he could feel her eyes on him, he turned and stared back at the castle.

She opened the window and waved, and he lifted his hand. It was as if he'd reached out and touched her, and she felt the warmth of his greeting down to her bones.

'Mum? Are you awake?'

She closed the window and turned to hug Jenni, bleary-eyed and sleepy, in so many ways still her little girl. 'How are you, darling? Did you sleep well?'

'Mmm. Still sleeping.'

Maisie laughed and hugged her tighter. 'Silly girl. Excited?'

'Very.' She dropped her arms and took Maisie's hand. 'Come on, I want a cup of tea, and we need to start moving. It's only two hours before the hairdresser comes, and I want to do my nails and make sure I've got everything ready.'

'Are the girls awake?'

'Yes, I called them. They're making tea in the kitchen with Grannie and Jeff, but I wanted you to come. Where's Dad?'

'Walking the dogs.'

He got back while they were all in the kitchen making toast, and joined in, apparently quite at ease with three young women in scanty vest tops and sloppy pyjama trousers. He probably was, to be fair, now that Jenni lived here permanently. And if anyone needed to be self-conscious, she thought, it was her, dressed much the same except that she'd thrown a light robe over the top, and now she was glad she had, because his eyes kept straying to her all the time.

'More toast, anyone?' Helen said, but they all shook their heads.

'No, thank you, Grannie. I need a shower,' Jenni said.

'Mmm, me too,' Maisie agreed, and then caught a flash of heat in Rob's eyes and turned away quickly before he could see the wash of colour across her cheeks.

'I'll go and check everything's under control outside,' he said, and left the room, to Maisie's relief. Mrs McCrae bustled in and hugged Jenni, her eyes filling with tears, and Jenni hugged her back hard, making Maisie's eyes fill as well.

Oh, dear lord, it was going to be one of those days, she realised with a bubble of hysterical laughter in her throat, and almost ran back to her room before it escaped on a wave of tears. She showered and washed her hair, taming it with serum and scrunch-drying it. There was no point asking the hairdresser to deal with it. She'd had almost forty years of learning how to control the wild curls, and she didn't want to look like someone else on such an important day.

She threw on clean clothes and went to see how Jenni was coping, and got swept up in the preparations. The hairdresser arrived, someone opened a bottle of champagne, Mrs McCrae brought up a tray of bagels with cream cheese and smoked salmon, and Jenni's room turned into party central. Jeff was recording it all for posterity, moving unobtrusively around the room as he photographed the dress, the shoes, the girls laughing, the pinning up of Jenni's hair—all the little details that otherwise would be lost.

She wondered what Rob was doing, and then saw him out of the window talking to the florist. She went out to join them, checked that everything was all right, that the table centres were where they should have been, that the pedestals were in the right places, and then she looked at Jenni's bouquet and her eyes filled with tears.

'Oh, it's lovely! Thank you so much!'

It was cream and white, with just a touch of lilac to take the edge off, for Helen's sake, and echo the bridesmaids' posies. So pretty, so perfect for her little girl's special day.

'Hey, come on, you can't start already,' Rob said gruffly, and slung an arm round her shoulders, hugging her to his side. She slid her arm round his waist and hung on.

'She's my baby,' she said, her voice breaking, and he turned her into his arms and held her while she cried the tears that had been threatening for weeks.

When he let her go, she could see his own eyes bright with tears, the lashes clumped, and she gave him another quick hug and went up on tiptoe to kiss his cheek.

'Come on, soldier. We can do this.'

'Yes, we can,' he said, his voice steady and confident, and she had a feeling that he wasn't talking about the wedding at all, and she felt all the stress and worry fade away.

'How are you all doing?'

'OK, Helen. How about you? That looks really lovely,' Maisie said, smiling at her as she did a little twirl in her new outfit that they'd chosen together the last time she'd been here.

'Thank you. I feel so much better in it. Oh,

Jenni, you look beautiful. How long? Your father's pacing.'

'We'll be down in five minutes,' Jenni said, as the hairdresser anchored the veil into the back of her hair and stood back.

'Perfect. That's lovely.'

Lovely? Oh, yes, she was lovely, but so much more. She looked like a woman, serene, confident, sure of her love.

Maisie went out onto the landing, and the girls ushered Jenni out, arranging her dress and veil as they walked down the landing, Jeff firing off endless shots as they moved towards the head of the stairs. As Maisie turned the corner at the top of the stairs, she saw Rob standing there, one foot on the bottom step, his hand resting on the newel post, gazing up at them and looking for all the world like one of the oil paintings around the walls.

His silver-buttoned black jacket and waistcoat were straight out of history, a deep jade ruched tie picking up the colour in the Mackenzie dress kilt and the matching flashes on his black kilt hose, his ghillie brogues gleaming. He looked every inch the Laird, and she felt her heart swell with pride.

'Maisie,' he said, holding out his hand, and she went down to him, her heart in her mouth as his eyes raked over her and darkened. 'You look stunning,' he said under his breath as she reached him, and she lifted a hand and touched his cheek.

'So do you. Who would have known you had such good legs, Mackenzie?' she teased, and then, taking the last step, she turned and watched as Jenni came down the stairs, her eyes filling as she reached her father's side.

'Oh, Jenni,' he said gruffly, cupping her shoulders with gentle hands and kissing her cheek. 'You look…'

He couldn't finish, couldn't say the words. There weren't words for how he felt at that moment, not words he could ever find.

'Don't you start, or you'll set me off,' she warned him, and he laughed softly and took a step back.

'Come and see your flowers. They're beautiful.'

'Oh, they are! Oh, Mum, look!'

'I know, I've seen.'

Seen and cried my eyes out, she thought, and then she noticed Rob wasn't wearing his buttonhole. 'Here, let me pin that on for you,' she said, taking it out of the box and reaching up with trembling fingers to pin it in place.

He returned the favour, his hands steady, his brow creased in a little frown of concentration. 'How's that?' he asked, and she looked down at it and smiled.

'Perfect. Thank you.'

'Right. You and Helen had better go,' he said, and opening the front door he helped them into the first of the three wedding cars waiting on the drive. It was only a short journey to the church; they could have walked, but the weather was never reliable enough for that and, besides, with her stomach in knots and her legs like jelly, she wasn't sure she would have made it.

The church was packed with family and friends, many of them people she'd never met, but Helen greeted them all, introducing her to one or two, and Maisie held her head high and smiled through the speculative glances.

Alec came up to her, his hands shaking as he took hers and kissed her cheek, and she hugged him and told him not to worry.

'How's Jenni?' he asked, and she smiled.

'Beautiful. She can't wait.'

'Nor can I.'

He went back to his place at the front of the church, and she waved to the Coopers, sitting behind their son, Seonaid's hat a delicate confection of lavender, toning with her husband's tartan. She looked nervous, and Maisie winked at her in solidarity, and then turned back to see if her brother had arrived.

And stopped in her tracks, because her father was there too, his face stern. She went over to him, wondering how much more emotion she was going to feel today, and he took her hand in his and gave what passed for a smile. 'I couldn't let my granddaughter get married without seeing her off,' he said.

Why not? He hadn't seen her off, Maisie thought, but she didn't say that, she just thanked him for coming and wondered where they'd seat him. With her brother Peter and his wife, of course, she thought, and greeted them distractedly.

'I'll catch up with you later. The bridesmaids are here, so Jenni won't be far behind. I'd better sit down,' she said, and took her place beside Helen, her heart pounding.

Then the music changed, and with her heart in her mouth she turned to watch as the man who once had waited for her where Alec was standing now walked their daughter down the aisle to the man she loved with all her heart.

Her eyes were shining, her face alight with happiness, and Rob, with his hand over hers in the crook of his arm, walked her slowly down past Maisie and took his place in front of the minister.

When he'd given her hand to Alec, he moved into the pew beside her and she felt his hand brush hers. Their fingers linked and clung, and together they watched as Alec and Jenni made their vows.

The same vows she and Rob had exchanged, the

vows that had counted for nothing in the face of all that was to come. But that had been long ago, and really nothing had changed.

She still loved him. There had been no one else for her, and never would be. He was her husband still in everything but law, and if he asked her again, she would marry him once more, would say these vows to him again and mean them, from the bottom of her heart…

The reception seemed to go on forever.

Rob had made his speech, caused a few chuckles and brought tears to the eyes of his daughter and the woman who should still have been his wife. He'd laughed at Alec's speech, laughed even more at the best man's, and best of all he'd got through it all without losing it.

But now the first dance was over, and he could hear the unmistakeable sound of a helicopter in the sky above.

'Whatever's that?' Jenni said, turning to Alec on the dance floor as the music stopped, and Rob and Maisie led them all outside to the lawn and they watched the helicopter land, settling like a feather on the circular lawn up above the castle.

'Dad? What's that?' Jenni asked, and he pulled a face and grinned.

'Your going-away car.'

'But—we're not going away,' Alec said, looking puzzled. 'We haven't packed.'

'Yes, you have,' his mother said, and his father handed the pilot his bag.

'Here,' Tricia said, handing over Jenni's. 'Blame Libby if there's anything missing.'

'But—where are we going?' Jenni asked, so he told them, and their jaws dropped.

'Wow—Dad?'

'Come here,' he said, and she flew into his arms, still his little girl, but not for long. He let her go, handed her over to her husband, slapped Alec on the back and then showered them both with confetti as they ran towards the helicopter. Her veil took off, and Alec grabbed it and bundled it up and helped her into the little aircraft, turning to wave as they took their seats.

And then they were gone, lifting up into the sky, and Rob watched them, Maisie's hand in his, until they were nothing more than a dot on the horizon. Then he turned to her.

'I think we've got a party to host,' he said, and she smiled at him through her tears, swiped them out of the way with an ineffectual hand and turned back to their guests.

CHAPTER TEN

So, it was done.

Her baby was married, whisked away on her honeymoon with tears in her eyes and love in her heart, and now the party was over.

She'd danced for hours, until her feet could hardly hold her, the ceilidh band loud and lively and endless as the caller had kept them all in order and they had laughingly gone wrong anyway. The dashing white sergeant had dashed away, the willow had been stripped within an inch of its life, and they'd finished off with the old Orcadian version of stripping the willow, with two long lines of men and women, crossing and recrossing, whirling each other round until they were giddy and helpless with laughter, and then they'd all joined hands for 'Auld Lang Syne'.

And now the house was quiet, the air still but for a light breeze, and Maisie took herself out to the gun court, rested her hands against the ancient stone wall and stared out over the moonlit sea.

'I thought I might find you here.'

She turned her head, looking at him over her shoulder. 'Have they all gone?'

He nodded. 'I've just seen my mother up to bed. She's exhausted.'

'I'm sure. Do you need to walk the dogs?'

'No. They had a run earlier, one of the ushers took them out. I'll give them a good walk tomorrow, but they're sleeping now.'

He fell silent, the tension between them palpable.

'It was a good day,' she said finally, just to break the silence, and he came and stood beside her, staring out over the sea, his face pale in the moonlight.

'Yes, it was. Better than I thought it would be.'

'They looked thrilled with the helicopter. That was very generous of you.'

He shrugged. 'They aren't having long off, it's a very short break, but I just felt I wanted them to have a little privacy. The gatehouse isn't exactly a honeymoon hideaway and they've waited a long time for this.'

She felt a pang of motherly concern, thinking back to their first night together, and Rob's tenderness and patience. Would Alec be as kind with Jenni?

'He'll take good care of her,' he said gruffly, as

if he could read her thoughts. 'He adores her, Maisie. She'll be fine.'

'I know. Your speech was lovely, by the way,' she told him. 'Very touching.'

'I made you cry.'

She laughed, a breathless little sound in the quiet night. 'It wasn't hard.'

'No. It's been a bit of an emotional roller-coaster.' He turned her towards him, staring down at her, his eyes shadowed. 'You looked beautiful today,' he murmured. 'I love that dress.'

'I love it, too. Jenni said—'

She broke off, thinking too late that it might not be wise to tell him what Jenni had said, but he just smiled and tilted his head curiously.

'What?' he prompted.

'She said it would blow your socks off.'

He laughed softly, then gave a quiet sigh. 'How very true.' He turned away again, staring out to sea, his eyes unfocused, remembering Maisie dancing, the sway of her hips, the way she'd doubled up with laughter until she could hardly breathe. It wasn't the dress that had blown his socks off, it was the woman he loved, the woman he should never have allowed to slip through his fingers. Did he dare to try to win her love once more?

'Maisie, I don't know if I can do this again,' he confessed softly, finally voicing the thoughts he'd had all day. 'I've held on all these years, never married again, never even got close, but now you're back here and it feels as right as it could, but even so, I'm afraid to let myself trust it.'

He breathed in deeply, then let his breath out on a harsh, ragged sigh. 'What if I'm wrong, Maisie? What if you come back here and find you still hate it after all? What if I let you back into my heart, and you leave me all over again?'

'I don't hate it,' she said quietly. 'I don't think I ever really did hate it. I hated being lonely, I hated being without you, and I had no friends, but I was never unhappy with you, Rob. I was only unhappy without you, or when you held yourself back from me. And when I left because I couldn't stand it any more, you didn't come after me. I thought you would, thought you'd come to Cambridge on leave, so we could have a chance to work on our marriage, but you didn't. Only to visit Jenni, and then not for six months.'

'I couldn't,' he told her. 'I was so confused, so hurt, so angry. My parents gave me your letter when I got back, told me you'd left me. I was devastated. I thought it was better to leave it for a while, to let things settle, then maybe we'd be able to talk. I think I was waiting for you to realise you'd made a mistake and come back to me, but you didn't, and why should you? And I'm not going to blame my parents. They didn't help, but I should have talked to you, should have realised something was wrong. I should have come after you.'

'I wrote to you again, weeks later when I knew you were home, but you didn't answer my letter. You didn't even acknowledge it.'

'I never got a letter,' he said, and he shook his head slowly, his expression resigned. 'My father.'

'Not necessarily. Things get lost.'

His smile was wry. 'No, Maisie. They don't.' He sighed softly, his expression bleak now. 'I know I've let you down, but I still love you, Maisie, more now, maybe, than I did then, because I know now what I've lost.'

She closed her eyes, breathing slowly, steadying her heart. He still loved her. Nothing else mattered—only that. She reached up and cradled his face, turning it gently towards her. 'Rob, after the food tasting, when you kissed me and I stopped you, you said you'd never wanted to hurt me, it was just the wrong time for us. But it's the right time now. I don't want to hurt you, either. I love you, too, Rob. I've never stopped loving you. I just couldn't live here without you, and I was faced with another five years of that. I never left you. When you asked for a divorce, I was devastated.'

He stared at her. 'I thought that was what you wanted?'

'No. I wanted you, Rob. I've only ever wanted you, but I was too young to know how to tell you that, too young and inexperienced and proud to fight for you. But it's different now. We're different now—older. Wiser.'

She took a deep breath for courage and held his eyes.

'Ask me again, Rob. Ask me now.'

He looked around, looked at the lights still on in some of the guest rooms, and shook his head. 'Not here. Not like this. Meet me here in five minutes— and you might want to change your shoes.'

The ruin. He was taking her to the ruin, the place where they'd always gone to be alone. The place where Alec had asked Jenni to marry him only ten weeks ago.

She went inside and slipped off her shoes, then ran up to her bedroom. How quickly could she shower?

Very, was the answer. She pulled on clean underwear, and then because he loved the dress, because he'd suggested she change her shoes, and only shoes, she put it back on again, zipped it up and put on her little flat gold pumps, the ones she wore with her jeans.

Then she ran back down to the gun court and found him waiting, still in his kilt, but he'd lost the jacket and waistcoat and tie, the shirt was undone at the neck and he had a wicker hamper in one hand and a blanket over his shoulder.

'Ready?' he asked, and she nodded, slipped her hand into his and squeezed it tight, then they went down the worn stone steps to the beach, along the shore with the suck of the sea in the shingle for company, picking their way carefully but hurrying nonetheless because after all this time the suspense was killing them both.

The moon was bright, lighting their way along the familiar path, but Rob led her, turning every now and then to make sure she was all right, helping her up steps, over rocks, round the rough patches.

And when they reached the ruins of the old castle, he led her gently by the hand to their crumbled tower in the corner overlooking the sea, and he spread out the blanket on the ground, knelt down on it and held out his hand to her, drawing her down to him.

She knelt in front of him, just inches away from him, and he took her hand in his, his eyes steady on hers even though she could see a pulse hammering in his neck.

'I love you, Maisie,' he began. 'I've loved you since the first moment I saw you, and I wish with all my heart that I'd been able to make things right for you, that I'd had the courage to come and find you, the humility to ask you to have me back, instead of hiding away up here and throwing away so much that was good and precious in our lives. But I didn't, and I lost you, but I've never forgotten you, not for a moment.'

She felt a tear slide down her cheek, and brushed it away, and he lifted his hand and smoothed the last trace from her skin with a hand that wasn't quite steady.

'There have been other women,' he went on softly. 'Redheads at first, but they weren't you, so I switched to blondes and brunettes, and then I realised I was cheating all of us, I was sick of pretending, sick of shutting my eyes so I could convince myself it was you, ashamed that I was using women, nice, ordinary, decent women, to forget you. And it didn't work anyway, so I stopped. It was easier that way, less painful, and it meant I could look at myself in the mirror in the morning when I shaved. But I hated it, because I'd vowed to be faithful to you for the rest of our lives, and we'd thrown it all away.

'But I want it back, my love. I want you back, and if it means I have to fly down every weekend and divide my time between here and Cambridge to do it, then so be it, because when you went away this time, the life went out of the Highlands for me. I got through it, but all I could think about was when you'd be coming back and how long it would be until I could see you again. The castle's nothing without you, just a pile of rock on the edge of the sea somewhere just shy of the Arctic Circle.'

She smiled at that, but it was a poor effort, a wobbly smile that turned somehow into a tiny sob, and he squeezed her hand and pressed it to his lips. 'I understood then what you meant about living here without me; I was just getting through the days till you returned, my life suspended. It was like being in a coma, going through the motions, but nothing seemed real—even the wedding preparations hardly scratched the surface. And I began to realise what it must have been like for a young woman, alone, friendless, with a small, demanding baby and no one to turn to, no one to hold you or tell you it would get better. No one to love you.'

'I thought you loved me,' she said sadly, confused. 'But when you came back, you were so different. All I wanted was a hug, but you didn't come near me.'

'I was afraid to hurt you, afraid of my emotions. I wanted you so much—I'd been shut up under the sea in a metal tube for months, and the thought of holding you, making love to you again, was all that got me through. And I didn't trust myself.'

'You should have said—'

'We both should have said. It wasn't just that. Maybe that was just a good excuse. I was really unhappy in the navy, but when I came home and needed you to hold me and tell me I'd get through it, you were so wrapped up in Jenni and so obviously unhappy I just had to bury my own problems and concentrate on yours. But I couldn't. I wasn't mature enough to do it, and so I lost you.'

Tears were coursing down her cheeks now, but she just blinked them away. 'I'm so sorry. I didn't realise what you were going through. That must have been so awful.'

'Well, you know the saying, "What doesn't kill you makes you stronger". I survived it, and it made me a better man, in the end, but the cost, to both of us, to Jenni, just doesn't bear thinking about. The children we might have had. The time together, for the last twenty years—so much, just gone. And I don't want to waste any more of our lives, Maisie. I need you. I love you. Come back to me, my love. Marry me again—and this time, let's do it right.'

'Oh, Rob…' She sucked in a shaky breath, and fell into his arms, the tears falling like sweet summer rain, washing away the hurt.

His lips touched her cheeks, kissing away the salty trails, his thumb smoothing them out while he fought to hold back tears of his own. 'Yes or no, Maisie. Tell me now, for pity's sake.'

'Yes. Oh, yes, my love,' she said, lifting her face to his so he could see the love there for him, shining silver in the moonlight. 'Of course I'll marry you again, and I don't care where we live. I love it here, so long as you're here with me. I can still do my photography, and I can write features and send them to magazines and newspapers, if I want, or I could just help you here, help you to build up the business, work alongside you, if you want me.'

'Want you?' He laughed a touch crazily. 'Oh, my dearest, darling Maisie, of course I want you. I can think of nothing more wonderful than having you by my side every day of my life.'

'My family are down there. My father came, even after all the things that have been said, even though he's old and ill, he still cared enough to come to Jenni's wedding. I'll need to spend some time down there. And I've got other friends. Good friends who've stood by me. I can't forget them.'

'I wouldn't want you to. And, anyway, I've got the business in London and I go down from time to time, as you know, so we can keep the house in Cambridge as a base and go down together, and you can catch up with your friends and family while I keep my firm on the straight and narrow. And now we can leave this place with Jenni and

Alec, it's not such a problem to get away. It's going to be theirs, after all. And my mother might like to spend some time in Cambridge, and Jenni and Alec. It won't go to waste. Talking of which…'

He drew her gently into his arms, kissed her tenderly, then shifted so he was sitting down, one leg bent at the knee. He patted the rug beside him and she settled there, watching as he opened the hamper and pulled out a bottle and two glasses, a little basket of canapés left over from the wedding and a big chunk of Mrs McCrae's fruit cake.

'What are you doing?'

'Feeding you. I don't know about you, but I hardly ate anything, I was too wound up, and I'm starving. Champagne?'

She started to laugh, and he gave a chuckle, then put the bottle down and lay back, laughing till the tears ran down his cheeks, Maisie cradled against his chest.

She lifted herself up on one elbow when she could breathe again, and stared down at his beloved face. 'Make love to me, Mackenzie,' she said softly. 'I've waited such a long, long time.'

'And you're going to have to wait a little longer,' he told her, kissing the tip of her nose before sitting up and reaching for the champagne. 'I'm taking a leaf out of our daughter's book, and doing it properly this time round. Only I'm not waiting

two and a half months. We're getting married in
two and a half weeks, my darling, so pull up a
glass, get stuck into the food and start planning.'

She wore the dress again, with the fascinator she'd
worn for Jenni's wedding as a veil, the net over
her face hiding her eyes from him as she walked
down the aisle on Alec's arm.

Jenni was behind her, waiting to take the simple
posy she had made of flowers from the castle
garden, and Helen and the Coopers and Mrs
McCrae made up the party.

Or that was the idea, but word had got out that
the Laird was marrying his lady again, and the
church was packed to the rafters, all the estate
workers up in the Laird's loft above them, anyone
who could get inside crowded in around the back
of the nave, and the rest were outside, cheering
and waving as she walked in to marry the man of
her dreams.

As she reached his side, he held out his hand to
her, his eyes glowing with love, and she went to
him with a smile that came from the heart. Their
vows were the same they'd made all those years
ago, but this time they said them with new convic-
tion, a deep-seated sincerity that left the other in
no doubt that this time their love was unshakeable.

He slipped the ring on her finger, the same ring

he'd put on nearly twenty-two years ago, and then she gave him his, a new one because he'd thrown his own into the sea in a rage of despair when their divorce had come through.

And then he kissed her, his eyes warm with the promise of what was to come, and after they'd signed the register, witnessed by Jenni and Alec, they turned and walked back down the aisle and out of the church together, arm in arm, in a hail of confetti and good wishes. He kissed her again, just to give the crowd something to make them happy, and then with a smile and a wave he led her away, down to the hotel where they were having a lunch party.

She could hardly eat anything. Her nerves were strung tight, her heart was racing, and every time he caught her eye, she knew he felt the same.

As if he'd read her mind, he passed on coffee and got to his feet, holding out his hand to her. 'Sorry to bail out on you, guys, but we're off now.'

'Off?' Alec said, his face a picture, but Rob just laughed.

'You'll cope. We'll be back the day after tomorrow. We've been waiting twenty years for this day, and I think you'll agree we've earned it.'

'Oh, Mum…'

Jenni got to her feet and hugged her, Alec too, and then they left the table, with Mrs McCrae dabbing her eyes and Helen trying to look disapproving and failing dismally, and he ushered her out to the car, which was waiting in the car park.

'So where *are* we going?' she asked, taking off the fascinator and dropping it down behind her seat as he put down the roof.

'The place we sent Jenni and Alec. We've got a lodge in the grounds, with a hot tub and room service.'

Her heart rate hitched up a gear, and she rested her head back as he drove swiftly through the glorious scenery, pulling up after a couple of hours outside a beautiful old country house hotel on the shores of a loch. They checked in, and the receptionist asked if they wanted to book dinner.

'No,' he said firmly. 'We'll get room service.'

And the moment the door was closed behind them, he drew her gently into his arms and stared down into her eyes. Then he lifted his hand and cradled her face.

'I love you, Mrs Mackenzie,' he said gruffly, and, lowering his head, he touched his lips to hers in a kiss of promise.

He lifted his head, and she reached up and laid her hand against his cheek, relishing the feel of stubble against her palm, the contrast between them, yin and yang. 'I love you, too,' she said, her heart slowing now because there was no hurry.

They had all the time in the world, and from the look of him, Rob intended to take it.

He crossed to the window and tilted the blinds, and the ring she'd put on his finger in their simple ceremony caught his eye. It felt strange after all these years, but he'd get used to it. And for now it was a constant reminder of what he'd so nearly lost. He'd thrown the other ring away, but this one he knew he would never take off, because it was engraved inside, with one simple word.

Forever…

* * * * *

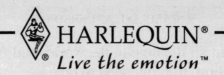

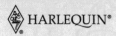

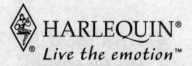

HARLEQUIN®
INTRIGUE®

BREATHTAKING ROMANTIC SUSPENSE

Shared dangers and passions lead to electrifying romance and heart-stopping suspense!

Every month, you'll meet six new heroes who are guaranteed to make your spine tingle and your pulse pound. With them you'll enter into the exciting world of Harlequin Intrigue— where your life is on the line and so is your heart!

THAT'S INTRIGUE— ROMANTIC SUSPENSE AT ITS BEST!

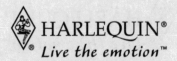

HARLEQUIN®
Live the emotion™

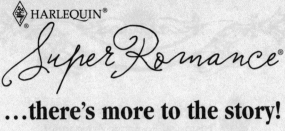

HARLEQUIN®
SuperRomance®

...there's more to the story!

Superromance.
A *big* satisfying read about unforgettable
characters. Each month we offer *six* very different
stories that range from family drama to adventure
and mystery, from highly emotional stories to
romantic comedies—and much more! Stories
about people you'll believe in and care about.
Stories too compelling to put down....

Our authors are among today's *best* romance
writers. You'll find familiar names and talented
newcomers. Many of them are award winners—
and you'll see why!

If you want the biggest and best
in romance fiction, you'll get it
from Superromance!

Exciting, Emotional, Unexpected...

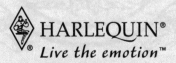

HARLEQUIN®
Live the emotion™

Harlequin® Historical
Historical Romantic Adventure!

*Imagine a time of chivalrous
knights and unconventional ladies,
roguish rakes and impetuous
heiresses, rugged cowboys
and spirited frontierswomen—
these rich and vivid tales will
capture your imagination!*

*Harlequin Historical…
they're too good to miss!*

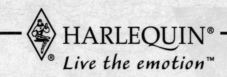

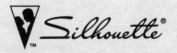